SECOND CHANCES
Kristen Rodgers

Publishers Note:
This is a work of fiction. All names, characters, places, and events are the work of the author's imagination. Any resemblance to real persons, places, or events is coincidental.

Cover Art: **Val Muller**

Copyright **Kristin Rodgers** ©2014
All rights reserved
ISBN 13: 978-0692328040
ISBN 10: 0692328041

www.dancingwithbearpublishing.com

~ ONE ~

Breathe, she thought. *One, two, three, four...*

Hannah held her head between her knees while balancing on the edge of the tub, ignoring the cold droplets of water that soaked through her jeans. The room swayed and black dots floated in front of her eyes.

It couldn't be true. Raising her head slightly, she peered over the counter at her reflection, trying to make herself believe it was a faulty result. But there it was, staring her dead in the eyes, two bright pink lines as clear as the blue skies outside. Standing, Hannah leaned over the sink and splashed cool water on her face.

Get it together. Her fears confirmed, she snatched the hand towel and patted her face. Of course she'd suspected it. There had been bouts of morning sickness, her stomach churned at the slightest smell of coffee and perfume—things that never bothered her before. There was also the fatigue that seemed to never go away and her constant craving for peanut butter. Her instincts rewound to the one night she hadn't played it safe and she felt an overwhelming sense of panic.

Choking back tears, Hannah paced the bathroom, trying to put things into perspective. Having arrived home from college an hour earlier, she already felt the burden of life after graduation. It was all happening too fast and not at all how she'd planned.

"Okay," she muttered to herself. "Think. Think. First things first..." *Tell Dad.* He was the only family she had. Since she'd just moved back into his house, it wasn't likely she could hide her secret for long.

She took a deep breath and headed for his office, stomach twisting in anticipation. She felt like a teenager again, about to confess that she got written up at school, instead of the young woman she was, in the predicament she now faced. But disappointing her dad wasn't something she'd done often, and on the rare occasion she did, she'd spent weeks trying to make up for it. Once, as a freshman in high school, she'd been caught copying her friend, Erin's math homework. As a result, the teacher gave her the first and only zero Hannah had ever gotten in her school career. Her dad had said nothing more, other than to tell her he was disappointed by her conduct, but for weeks she saw it in his eyes. This, she had the feeling, was going to take much longer.

Standing in his office doorway, Hannah tried to summon the courage to enter the room. It was a futile attempt because it wasn't likely she'd ever work up the nerve to face him. As if sensing her presence, her dad swiveled on the black chair and the leather moaned in protest. Glasses balanced on the bridge of his nose, he smiled while he studied her.

"Hey, hon," he said. "What's up?"

Hannah swallowed hard, noting how dry her mouth suddenly became. Over her hammering heart, she said, "I-I need to talk to you about something."

"Uh-oh," he teased, "sounds serious."

She stared unblinking. The furrow between his brows told her he sensed his comment hit home. He frowned, but cleared the overflowing mess of papers and books off the chair beside his desk.

"Okay, let's hear it," he said, and motioned for her to sit.

She took a deep, shaky breath and stared at her feet. "Something, uh, something has happened." Shaking her head, Hannah searched for words that would make the news less shocking.

His furrowed brow became a worried frown. "You're worrying me."

Just spit it out and get it over with. "I... I'm pregnant."

Hannah felt as though the bottom was falling out of her world. Her mind raced a mile a minute with a thousand *if-onlys.* Suddenly, she felt herself spinning out of control, teetering on the edge of a bottomless pit that threatened to swallow her. The life she'd known was gone, and soon enough she'd fade into a world filled with regret. A world of single parenting, and support groups where she would slowly become invisible until she disappeared altogether. Her new life would center on the baby and as it grew, she would pray it wouldn't make the same mistakes. She'd spend her years wishing for do-overs to make everything right again, while wistfully dreaming of the life she passed up.

Somehow, Hannah overcame the feeling that she was going to faint and snapped back to the present, to her father. At first, Hannah worried he'd stopped breathing. His stare was unwavering, as if he were waiting for a punch line that would never come. Then his jaw tensed and he ran a trembling hand through his hair. After tucking his glasses into one shirt pocket, her father pressed fingertips into his eyes and tiredly kneaded the wrinkled skin, letting the silence between them hover like a thick cloud. When he finally looked at her, his sharp gray eyes were clouded.

"Is it Ben's?" he asked at last.

Hannah slumped into the chair and hugged a pillow to her chest. Burying her face, she began to sob. She heard his exhausted sigh and the chair move, and then his arm wrapped around her shoulders.

"We'll get through this. We've gotten through worse." And then he stood and began to pace. "You'll see. Everything will be okay." He muttered a few inaudible words, his rambling unconvincing. Stopping in front of her, he asked, "How far along are you?"

Hannah shrugged, and dragged one sleeve of her sweatshirt across her eyes. "Couple of weeks. A month, maybe."

He sat beside her again and wrapped her in a comforting hug. "Have you told Ben?" His voice strengthened as the initial shock wore off.

9

Hannah bit her lower lip. "I told him my suspicions a couple of days before graduation. I couldn't bring myself to take a test to know for sure. I told him that I was probably feeling stressed from finals and the symptoms would pass." The tears began again, stronger this time. "And then I caught him with Stephanie that night."

"But... Stephanie? Your roommate, Stephanie? I thought you two were best friends."

Hannah swiped angrily at her tears and mumbled, "We were."

Her dad leaned forward, balanced both elbows on his knees and steepled his fingers under his chin. Hannah could almost read his mind. She was his heartbroken, scared little girl. It didn't matter to him that she'd turned twenty-three just a few months ago, or that she'd graduated from Florida State University with a degree in journalism. In his eyes, she'd always be his little girl.

"I don't imagine that was a peaceable confrontation."

In fact, Hannah hadn't dealt well with the situation at all. The betrayal of her best friend and boyfriend had caused something inside of her to snap. She'd handled it in a way that left her fearing she would be suspended, or even worse, denied graduation. However, the dean excused the incident and Hannah spared her father the worry she knew it would cause. She had bigger battles to fight. And those would be the ones her father's help would be invaluable.

Angry and hurt at the same time, Hannah said inhaled deeply, trying to control her emotions. "Let's just say we're through. For good."

She paused, the enormity of her situation weighing heavily, causing her to slump in the chair. Ben's rejection had left a gaping hole in her heart. For three years they'd been friends and lovers. Together, they'd shared great times and a few bad times. They shared friends, dreams, and their secret worlds. She thought he would always be

10

there for her despite the ups and downs they often endured. And aside from the callous fights and disagreements, they'd discussed marriage, a future together. Instead, Hannah discovered she actually meant little to him.

"What on earth am I going do with a baby?" she said, more to herself than her father.

Pulling her close, her father said, "No point worrying about it right now. We have plenty of time to figure things out."

"Don't worry about it? I'm broke, Dad, and I don't even have a job yet. The baby is going to—" The long list of items her child would need flashed in her mind. The crib, a high chair, plus bottles, diapers, tiny clothes... and not to mention medical care. Even if everything was perfect and normal, she would need prenatal care right off the top. And if she were lucky enough to find a job that paid more than minimum wage, there'd be daycare costs, formula, and babysitters. And no sleep, social life, or any free time ever again.

The feelings of losing control swept over her. How had she let her emotions ruin what she'd worked so hard to accomplish? She'd naively loved Ben, so much so, she'd compromised her future. Hands shaking and heart beating unusually fast, Hannah closed her eyes and tried to concentrate on her breathing. Anything to ease the panic beginning to choke her.

"Hannah, calm down, honey. All this fussing isn't going to get us anywhere." He stood in front of her, placed both hands on her shoulders and gave a reassuring squeeze. "We'll work it out. I promise."

For the first time in weeks, Hannah felt her dismay subside. Love and gratitude for her father flooded her as she looked into his eyes and saw his endless concern. Ever since her mother ran off to Florida eleven years ago to start a new life in the bars and clubs, he had been the only constant in her life, playing the part of both parents in raising a hormonal teenage girl. Through it all, he'd never

11

given up on Hannah's ambitions and wild ideas. Despite her shortcomings, he continued loving her.

Resting her head on her father's chest, she said miserably, "I'm sorry. About everything."

"Don't be sorry," he said, squeezing her once more. "C'mon, I'll help you take your stuff to your room." He stood, offered his hand, which she took with a smile. He squeezed her reassuringly, and then grabbed the two heaviest suitcases and headed upstairs to her room.
Hannah grabbed the last two suitcases, one in each hand and followed him.

He wasn't the tough soldier he used to be, she noted as his feet clomped tiredly up the steps. The only thing remaining of his Army days was the tight haircut and his stormy gray eyes. Fifteen years ago, he'd retired his military career for a church building and a congregation. He'd always told her he'd gotten off on the wrong foot, and that he should have started his life as a minister instead of a soldier. Giving orders was never his strong point but giving the gospel was.

When the Army denied his cross-train from Commander of the Airborne Battalion to Chaplain, he'd decided it was God's way of telling him to move on. So, with his military retirement, he'd opened a little chapel on the west side of town and became Reverend Michael Sinclair. Over the years the church grew with the little town of Linbeck, becoming a little chapel overflowing at the seams, straining to be the bigger vision Hannah's father always dared dream.

Maybe things would have turned out differently, she often thought, if he'd been the man he was when he'd opened the church. Maybe her mother would still be here, promising to love and nurture her grandbaby, to be by Hannah's side through it all.

But reality always played the darker hand. So here she was, with her dad, picking up the pieces of yet another life gone awry.

Michael deposited her bags just inside the door. He gestured toward the room. "Here you are. Everything exactly the way you left it."

Hannah glanced around. "It sure is. I have no idea how long I may need to stay. It could take me a while to get on my feet." Wincing, she added, "You sure that's all right?"

His brows rose and eyes widened. "Like I'd kick my pregnant daughter to the curb."

"What would I do without you?" She smiled and gave in to the impulse to hug him. Hannah threw her arms around him. "I promise not to be too big a pain. First thing in the morning, I'll start looking for a job, and once I have steady money coming in, I'll—"

He shook his head, interrupting her rambling. "Why don't you unpack while I get us something for supper? Tomorrow is soon enough to figure out the details."

As if on cue, the grandfather clock in the downstairs hall chimed. Six o'clock. Why did it feel more like midnight?

Michael turned to leave, then stopped, his hand still on the doorknob. "How does Tetrazini sound?"

Gratitude welled inside her. "Sounds great."

He grinned and shut the door behind him, leaving Hannah to reacquaint herself with the room of her youth.

She glanced around the sunny yellow room, taking in the paisley wallpaper, the frilly yellow comforter with its Swiss dots, the stuffed teddies, and splay of pictures. She hadn't been home in four years, she realized with a stab of guilt. Yet, as a poor college student, airfare between Florida and Illinois was far out of her budget. Her father had offered to fly her home on numerous occasions, but she wouldn't let him, not wanting to put a strain on an already tight budget. So, here she was, twenty-three and a college graduate, back in the room that held many of her adolescent memories. Looking at the framed photos made her cringe—braces, pimples, awkward growth spurts.

There, on the dresser, a photograph of her mother captured her attention. Crossing the room in three quick strides, she held it in shaking hands. Emotions welled inside her and she felt the familiar dull ache from her mother's years of absence. A rush of sadness clenched her stomach. The last day she'd spent with her mother had been one of the best she could remember.

For the first time in a long while, Hannah had woken up to a clear-eyed, smiling mother. Her breath hadn't smelled of booze, her words were crisp, and she'd seemed blissfully happy with the promise of a great day. Together they selected an outfit for Hannah—a purple sundress printed with small white flowers with pink buds. It'd been Hannah's favorite dress but the sound of her mother's praise made her feel like a princess.

They went to the movie *Drop Dead Fred*, which Hannah thought was hilarious. Afterward, they shared an ice cream cone from *Dairy Queen*, and Hannah remembered how her mother had spoiled her by ordering an extra scoop of chocolate on top. That evening, Hannah had gone to bed with a goodnight kiss and visions of the two of them spending every day like that one. But the next morning only brought an empty loneliness that Hannah quickly discovered was her mother's permanent replacement. She asked her dad where her mother was. The response was the lost, sad look that never left her father's eyes all these years later.

Snapping back to reality, Hannah found herself wondering if her mother's guidance and support would have led Hannah down a different path with a different ending. As she gazed at the smiling photo of her mother, Hannah realized how much she resented her for her selfishness and desertion. Opening a desk drawer, she tossed the picture inside with such force she heard the glass crack. With it out of sight, Hannah spotted another photo on her dresser.

She picked it up, a smile allowing her to push aside her anger. It was her best friend, Josh, in front of the gi-

14

raffes at the zoo. He'd been about fourteen at the time, with arms and legs too long and too skinny. A giraffe peered over the fence, its huge head nearly resting on Josh's shoulder as its long, slimy tongue licked his face. The look on Josh's face, disgusted but laughing.

Hannah sighed and placed the picture back on the dresser. Josh had been her best friend since they were five, having been neighbors their entire lives, and when school started, they'd gotten stuck in every grade together until high school.

She eyed the bottom drawer of her desk, knowing it was still overflowing with photos from those days long ago. Sliding it open, she grimaced at her second grade school picture smiling up at her. Even then her hair was thick and uncontrollable. The 1980's bangs hung in her green eyes and the gap between her front teeth had tormented her until she was twelve, grinned out from its frozen place in time. Hannah tossed it aside and rummaged in the drawer for pictures that promised better memories. She found a stack buried deep that made her smile and ache at once, wishing she could rewind to those bittersweet days.

They were from some of her earliest memories when she and Josh dug up earthworms, to sailing *Styrofoam* boats down their driveways in the melting snow. Pictures of the snowmen they built, the leaf piles they dove into, and their backyard camping adventures. Then, as they left childhood behind, there were pictures of the summer camps they attended, youth groups, and field trips. Memories flooded her mind. The two of them in their adolescence running with their group of friends, sneaking her mom's cigarettes to smoke them at the river, and sharing their first kiss. She looked at their high school days, remembering the parties, their prom, and other school events. She remembered tearing around town in Josh's rusted out '86 Cavalier, sighed and wiped a tear away.

There were no more pictures after high school, she realized sadly, peering into the empty drawer. Her scholarship to Florida State had taken her away from Linbeck and around the world as an exchange student, but she'd left her dad and Josh behind after graduation.

She did a quick mental calculation. It'd been four years since she'd last seen or talked to Josh, who, at one time had been like family to her. They'd spoken on the phone, Hannah recalled, and that final conversation had left her feeling happy but homesick. Shortly after, she began making friends and living the college life. Time passed and before she knew it, she graduated. Hannah shook her head, wondering how she'd let so much time fly by without a single thought or phone call to the ones that mattered most to her.

"Hannah, dinner's ready," her dad called from the kitchen.

Hunger pains sounded from her stomach as she quickly stacked the photos back in the drawer. Her legs protested as she stood, but the smell of dinner prompted her to head to the kitchen.

"Mmm," she said, breathing in deeply, thumping down the stairs. "It smells great."

"Take a seat, dear, take a seat," her dad said, gesturing to the two plates he'd arranged on the table.

Hannah eagerly sat and reached for the bowl of steaming food. Her dad shooed away her hand, and took his seat next to hers. "Hold your horses."

"Sorry, almost forgot." Then she reached over and gripped her dad's strong hand and bowed her head.

"Dear Lord," he began. "Thank you for bringing Hannah safely home. We pray for Your guidance and strength to get through this situation that seems difficult right now, and that one day You will show Hannah what a blessing You have given her. I also pray that through Your grace, You will help her to forgive Ben for the hurt he caused and that You will open his eyes to the responsibility he now has as a father. We believe You will see us through this and make us a stronger, happier family. Thank you for this food and this time we have together. In Jesus' Name. Amen."

Hannah blinked through the tears that had formed in her eyes. She squeezed her dad's hand.

He winked and said, "Shall we eat?"

"Yes. I can't wait any longer!"

Throughout dinner, they avoided the topic of Hannah's pregnancy. It was still too fresh, too painful, to talk about openly. Now that she'd shared her secret with her father, she felt no desire to stir it up again.

After they'd eaten and cleaned up, Hannah retreated to her room to unpack. She sat on the edge of her bed, looking at the room that held the girl she used to be, and the suitcases in front of her that contained the woman she'd become. She'd accomplished nearly every goal she spent her teenage years dreaming of, yet she still felt empty inside. Linbeck had released its hold on her temporarily, long enough for her to satisfy her need for adventure and excitement. Then it'd wrapped its claws around her throat and dragged her back, pregnant and completely alone.

Sighing, Hannah rummaged through her suitcases until she found her pajamas and toothbrush. It had been a long month, week, and day. She was home, safe within the four walls that cradled her through every occasion in life. Now exhausted, Hannah snuggled into the smothering warmth under the cave of blankets until she fell into a fitful sleep.

~ TWO ~

She awoke to dawn filtering through the opening between the curtain panels. Hannah opened her eyes and sleepily watched dust motes dance on golden beams of morning sun. She squinted at the clock and fell back onto the downy pillow, and groaned. "Six-thirty?"

Then a familiar, comforting aroma wafted through the air. Dad's special pancakes with bacon. She tossed the covers aside, yawned, and slipped into her robe. Her stomach rumbled as she hurried down the stairs.

"'Morning, Dad," she said, entering the kitchen.

"Good morning." He buttered a slice of toast. "And how's my college graduate?"

I'd be fine if there wasn't a baby growing inside me. I'd be fine if I had a job, a place of my own, and someone to go through this with, Hannah thought. Instead, she muttered, "Fine." Then loaded her plate.

Michael filled his coffee mug and carried it to the table and sat across from his daughter. "So tell me, what's on your schedule today?"

"Don't know," she said, forking a pancake. "Haven't gotten that far yet."

He opened the newspaper and laid it beside his plate. "Stop by the church later," he said, peering over his glasses. "Choir practice today."

Hannah felt wistful at the mention of choir practice. Before college it had been one of the only pastimes she'd been devoted to. She was often asked to perform solos, and one of her favorites was *Amazing Grace*, sung a cappella.

Admitting to herself that she missed those days, she said softly, "Maybe next practice." Then added quickly, so as not to upset her dad, "After I wash up our breakfast dishes, I'll check out the want ads."

Her father didn't look up from the paper when he

said, "It'll be nice having you around the house for a while. I'm sure you'll find a good job in time." When he met her eyes, Hannah noticed the hope in his eyes. "Couldn't hurt to come back to church, though. Might be what's missing."

How could he know that it seemed a huge, empty cavern had formed inside her?

"Can't blame me for worrying about you, hon. You've seemed so... lost since you quit going to church."

Hannah sighed. If only it were that easy. Go to church, say a prayer or two, and *poof*, all of her problems would disappear. "Sunday," she promised, "okay?"

He reached across the table and patted her hand. "Okay." Standing, he grabbed his keys and briefcase. "Nice of you to clean up. Saves me a few minutes, and I have a busy morning. Call if you need me. For anything."

With a faint smile and a half-hearted nod, Hannah sat at the table and listened to the quiet thump of his car door as it closed. The motor revved and then the battered Honda backed out of the driveway.

Linbeck, the stereotypical small town that boasted nothing. Nothing to do and nowhere to go. Now, after being away at college for four years, she didn't have any friends left to call. She regretted letting her relationship with Josh grow cold. He'd always been her confidant, her someone to go to and share a good laugh, or unload her burdens. Josh had a way of making everything seem better, and she was craving a taste of that.

Hannah rinsed the plates and loaded the dishwasher, then headed upstairs to take a shower. Standing under the soothing rush of hot water, she began wishing she could wash her problems down the drain too. If only she could scrub her life clean and start over fresh. A brief longing for her mother's comfort and advice flashed through her mind, but she shoved it away. Instead, she silently thanked God for her dad. She knew it had been difficult for him to stay silent about the baby this morning, but he'd refrained from pushing her to church too much. For that, she was grateful.

Twenty minutes later, she was back at the table, staring out the window with her chin in her palm. A flittering yellow butterfly circled the patch of Willow Asters her father planted year after year. She felt the restless urge sneak up on her again. Usually, when it appeared, Hannah would go hang gliding or rock repelling but there was none of that in Linbeck. College had been the perfect place for her addiction to excitement. Surrounded by friends, there was always someone to go along, to turn a boring day into an exhilarating one. She always suspected her desire for the wild and crazy was her way of running from her thoughts. Left alone too long, they bombard her brain, stirring up the past and anger that seemed to take root inside her after her mother left. But if she kept busy, if she defied death by living through her stunts, she felt like she was doing more than just existing. She felt alive.

Sighing, Hannah realized how selfish she was. She was going to be a mother, whether she liked it or not, and she needed to get back to reality. And that reality wasn't college life anymore. Feeling the sudden need for fresh air, Hannah put on her shoes and headed to the river near the edge of their land.

She noticed a well-worn path winding through the weeds that hadn't been there when she was growing up. She and Josh used to find their way to the bank by running in the general direction of the grove of Slippery Elms that suddenly sprang up from the earth. She remembered how those trees used to stretch above them, yawning into the sky and creating a canopy of leaves that shaded the rocks and the slow-moving waves where they skipped stones. The wind rolled through the trees, causing them to shiver and sway, sending the calming, rustling of their leaves through the air. As she came nearer, she saw not much had changed except for the path that rudely interrupted their slumber.

The night left behind a layer of dew glistening like gems in the sunlight while the freshly watered flowers dotting the riverbank perfumed the air. Hannah stood at the river's edge, her mind flushed with memories of happier times. Swimming with Josh during the day, and watching the stars blink in the inky black sky at night. When she spied the gnarled old oak where Josh had carved their initials, she remembered this was the spot where they had shared their first kiss. She felt herself blush at the memory and suddenly missed her best friend.

"Well, well, well." A familiar voice came from somewhere behind her. "If it isn't Baby Sinclair."

Smiling even before she turned around, Hannah's heart quickened. *Baby* had been his nickname for her from their very first viewing of the movie, *Dirty Dancing*.

"Josh Reynolds," she said, turning to face him, "the ghost of my past." Hannah's first thought at seeing him was how he'd grown since high school. His brown hair wasn't as short as it had been back then. Barely touching his collar, it was just long enough on top to look stylishly messy, and he sported sideburns and a neatly-trimmed goatee that made his tanned face look older and accented those emerald green eyes.

"A little birdie told me you were back in town," he said, heading down the hill toward her. "Had to see for myself." His lips slanted into a teasing grin. "Glad to see it's true."

Crossing both arms over her chest, Hannah said, "Exactly which *little birdie* spilled my secret?"

He stood directly in front of her and said, "Why, the great Reverend Michael Sinclair. Who else?"

Josh studied her face, and for a moment she worried he might see that she'd come home, humiliated, jobless, and pregnant. But before she could worry about it, he pulled her into a warm bear hug. Hannah returned the embrace, surprised at how good it felt to be in his arms. Stepping back to search his handsome face, Hannah smiled.

Stooping to pluck a weed and then roll it between his fingers, Josh said, "Stopped by your house after talking with your dad. When you weren't there, I knew exactly where to find you."

He had a strange expression on his face, something unfamiliar—one she couldn't describe. Surely, her father hadn't told him about the baby. Hannah could see him observing her, this unfamiliar girl that had grown up during their years apart. Growing up, there had never been anything about her that stood out. Not her uncontrollable brown hair, or her shapeless teenage body.

She remembered one boy she had dated for a week in high school, Dusty Wendell, who told her she had an alluring smile. His grades perfect and fancy use of words had been the only reason Hannah went out with him. So, to make up for her lack of beauty, she mastered flirting skills and became passionate about the valiant things in life. She also learned how to tame her hair.
Having since grown out of her awkwardness, her body finally that of a woman with curves instead of planes and angles, she wore her hair long and layered, with dark highlights making it look almost black.

Uncomfortable under his scrutiny, Hannah fidgeted nervously. "So what have you been up to?" She swatted at an annoying mosquito buzzing around her head.
"Your dad didn't tell you?"

The three years since they'd last spoken seemed to fly by. So eager to escape Linbeck, she selfishly allowed her life to be consumed by her new friends, new boyfriend, and new school. Now, she felt the shame of her actions burning inside her. "You haven't come up in conversations recently," she replied. But one look at his pained expression told her the intended joke had fallen flat.

Josh looked out over the river, the sunlight glinting from his long, dark lashes. "Yeah, right. I work for him." He picked up a stone, pitched it into the water. "I'm the youth pastor and I'm in charge of missions for the church."

Hannah felt her jaw drop and snapped it shut. "Youth pastor? Missions? You?" She giggled. "Okay, who are you, and what have you done with the Josh I used to know?"

22

He returned her smile. "You make it sound like a bad thing."

"No, of course it's not," she said. "It just that, um, none of this sounds like something my Josh would do." She gave him a playful shove. "So when did you go all holy on me?"

The bright green of his eyes darkened. "While you were off running around Europe," he said flatly.

There was no mistaking the hint of bitterness she heard in his voice. Squaring her shoulders, she quoted him. "You make it sound like a bad thing."

"Nah. Not bad, exactly. But...." Josh shrugged. "I lost my best friend."

Staring at the ground, Hannah shuffled weeds with her foot. "Guess I got a little...." Self-centered? "A little busy." Awkward silence filled the air. Birds sang and crickets chirped, and the river continued to roll past.

Finally, Josh cleared his throat. "You want to head back to your house? It's getting a little warm out here."

Warm in more ways than one, she thought, pressing both hands to her cheeks.

They turned and headed down the beaten path. Hannah tromped through the weeds behind Josh, swatting the air at an attacking cloud of mosquitoes. "Do tell me, Josh. How does one go from a business major to a youth pastor and missionary?"

He smiled at her over his shoulder, his teeth glimmering against his tanned skin and dark hair, causing butterflies to take flight in her stomach. *Funny*, she thought, *he never had this effect on me while we were growing up.*

"Pretty simple, actually. I spent the entire spring break of freshman year partying so hard I barely remember it. The day before classes started up I was so hung over, I couldn't even get out of bed. Made me wonder what I was doing. I mean, what was the point? Why was I here? I started asking all those questions everyone asks at some point in their lives." He shrugged. "I don't know. But I was miserable and going nowhere. Fast."

Hannah understood completely. She'd felt the same way over the years, dozens of times but always shoved the thoughts aside, thinking it was easier to keep living as she was than make the necessary changes. Though, to be honest, she still didn't know what those changes might be.

"So later that day," Josh continued, "I ran into your dad. We started talking, and he invited me to church. It'd been so long since I'd been there, or to any church, for that matter, but I agreed to go. And that Sunday, I rededicated my life to the Lord. Michael offered me a summer job a couple of months later, and I decided not to go back to college for business. I got my teaching degree instead, and while I was in school, he offered me the position of youth pastor. Voila, here I am."

"Voila?" She couldn't believe her ears. While she admired him, Hannah couldn't help feeling regret that she hadn't stayed closer to home. Maybe her own life would have taken a similar turn. "That's it? You went to church one day, changed your major the next, and became a youth pastor?"

"Yeah, that's pretty much how it was." Josh laughed. "We have an affiliate church in New York and we donate funds to their mission program. A few opportunities came up, enabling me to go on some missions to help those in need, so I've spent a couple of years doing that, too."

"You're telling me that you, the guy who hated mowing lawns and raking leaves and shoveling snow, enjoys building huts and reading the Bible to the poor?"

"There is a little more to it than that," he replied dryly.

"I have to admit," she said, as they approached the house, "it's hard to picture you doing that kind of stuff." By now they were both sweating. "Would you like a drink?" Hannah offered, reluctant to end their conversation..

"Water would be excellent," Josh replied, shoving his hands in his pockets.

Hannah quickly retrieved two waters from the refrigerator and joined Josh outside again. "How about we relax
a minute on the porch?"

"Sure," Josh said, following her up the front steps
where they both claimed seats and opened their bottles of
water. In the silence of their first drinks, Hannah wondered
if she should tell him about Ben and the baby. She quickly
decided against it, though, sensing it was a little too much
information for a reunion meeting. There would be a better
time... at least she hoped she'd be given the opportunity to
salvage their friendship.

"Your turn," Josh said, settling deeper into the
bentwood rocker.

She'd been his best friend for so long, she thought for
sure he would have kept up through her father. Feeling
slightly hurt, Hannah hid her feelings behind a smile. "So,
my father and my best friend never discussed me, not once
in all these years?"

"We had more important things to worry about than
your latest adventure." Again, the tinge of anger.

Hannah remembered the year she studied in Germa-
ny, then backpacked through Europe with half a dozen college friends. Upon returning to the States, she felt worldly
and wise, and so grown up. Amazing how maturity can
mask itself in so many ways.

She took a sip of water and swirled it around in her
mouth before swallowing. At least one good thing came of
her school days: she managed to graduate with honors.
Hopefully, that fact would help her land a good job because she'd need quite a salary to support herself and her
baby.

How could she break the news to Josh? Maybe it was
best to let him find out on his own. Or maybe, she'd get a
job out of state, and be long gone before she started to
show. That idea was quickly doused at the thought of leaving her dad again. Hadn't she been the one to say it? What
would she do without him? One hand on her stomach, she

knew what she had done without his guidance.

Bringing herself back to the present, she said, "I'm sorry we lost touch. I was selfish and I should have—"

Josh cut her off with a wave of his hand. "No need to apologize, Hannah. It's history." He looked uncomfortable, but then added, "Now, why don't you tell me what you've been up to all these years?"

Hannah took a deep breath, wishing he would let her in but knowing it would take more time than a thirty-minute reunion. Instead of broaching the subject again, she gave Josh a brief rundown of her years away. Sugar-coating most of it, she managed to make herself sound nonchalant instead of arrogant or proud. She could sense Josh didn't think too highly of her at the moment, so she tried to avoid giving him any more reason.

At the end of Hannah's narrative, she turned the conversation back to him. "So, I don't see a ring on your finger... any prospects?"

Josh laughed. "No. Still going solo."

He didn't offer her much, but she couldn't help feeling pleased at the information. She knew she should be wishing the best for him, even if it meant him having met another girl. Still, as selfish as it sounded, Josh had always been hers. There had never been anyone else in all their years of friendship. Hiding her relief behind another sip of water, Hannah silently noted that Josh didn't seem too perturbed about still being single. She wished she could feel that kind of security about herself in knowing the right person would eventually come along. Instead, she'd taken matters into her own hands, which had gotten her nowhere.

"So," Josh said. "How about you?"

Hannah knew the question was coming, but dreaded it nonetheless. "Still looking," she said, trying to sound cheerful.

Josh nodded, allowing silence to stretch between them as he fingered his bottle and avoided her gaze. Hannah felt sad, remembering that at one time there'd never been awkward moments like this between them. She knew she was to blame for the state of their friendship but it still hurt.

Finally, standing, Josh said, "I'd better get going. It was good seeing you." Staring deep into her eyes, he added, "Really good."

Hannah didn't want him to leave. At least, not yet. She wanted to hear more about the man he'd become, and how he'd become that man. He was halfway down the sidewalk when she called to him. "You want to meet for lunch sometime? Finish catching up?"

"Yeah, sure. Why not?" Josh climbed into his car, his response noncommittal.

Hannah half-ran down the sidewalk and stopped beside the driver's door. "I'm glad you came to find me." She hoped he could see that she meant every word.

Despite his grin and friendly wink, sadness tinged his eyes. "Me too, Baby."

Hannah stepped back as he drove off in his old white Camaro, wishing their reunion had gone better. She sensed remorse from Josh and despite her natural urge to defend her actions, knew she had no right. She'd ditched him, point blank. Knowing how badly it hurt when Ben had done the same to her, Hannah could imagine how Josh felt, losing a best friend in such a cold-hearted way.

Back in the kitchen, she intended to make a peanut butter and jelly sandwich when she noticed a puddle of goo collecting on the refrigerator's bottom shelf. She set the jelly on the counter and grabbed a paper towel, scrubbing until the mess was gone. Hannah located a bottle of cleaner, quickly emptied the contents of the refrigerator and spritzed the shelves down. Finally satisfied that it was clean, she stocked the food and resumed making her sandwich. As she leaned against the counter to eat, Hannah spotted a dust ball in the corner. She frowned as she glanced at the floors, grimy and dotted with crumbs. Her heart ached seeing the mess, and she wondered what the rest of the place looked like.

She grabbed a paper plate and headed for the living room. For the first time since coming home, saw the clutter lining every bookshelf, a layer of dust on every piece of furniture, coffee and tea stains on the timeworn carpets. She slumped onto the couch as guilt shrouded her. It was obvious how much her father had needed her, yet he'd never so much as hinted at it.

The cold hard facts slapped her from self-pity. Yes, when her dad needed her most, she'd run off and left him alone without a thought. Just like her mother. How ironic that Josh had only left Linbeck to do good deeds and had a full, satisfying life to show for it, while she'd traveled the world and lived an adventurous life and came up empty-handed. Hannah suddenly realized she'd long ago used up her mother leaving as an excuse for her actions. That was no excuse for thinking she had rights and privileges, or to mistreat her father who, to give him his due, had done his best to be mother and father despite her attitude.

Hannah decided today was the day she turned over a new leaf and became the person she lost years ago. She'd start at the top, and clean until every windowpane sparkled and every countertop gleamed. When her dad came home for lunch, Hannah was on her hands and knees in the downstairs bathroom, scrubbing the tiles.

"What are you doing?"

"What does it look like? This place is a mess. How long has it been since you've cleaned?" Hannah rocked back on her heels.

"Couldn't tell you," he said, turning to go to the kitchen. "But keep it up. Looks great."

"Gee, thanks, Dad," she said, following him. "Guess who I saw today?"

"Who?" He rummaged through the contents in the refrigerator.

"Josh didn't tell you?"

28

"Should he have?" Her dad finally straightened with a container of leftovers in his hand and he glanced at her. "Lunch?"

Hannah shook her head and crossed her arms over her chest as she watched her dad load his plate full. "Why didn't you tell me he was working with you?"

"If I thought you cared, it might have come to mind." He slid his plate in the microwave.

The comment stung. And she had no right to question it. He was right, after all. Not once had she asked about Josh. Fact was, she'd never asked about her father, either. But that was old Hannah. New Hannah would behave differently.

She sat at the table. "Josh is mad at me, I think."

"What makes you say that?"

Hannah sighed. "Oh, just... everything." Tears stung at her eyes. "I'm sorry, Dad."

Raising his brow, he said, "For what? You called me a few times over the years."

She traced designs on the tabletop with her fingertip. "I left here thinking the world owed me an apology," she said, finally looking up at him. "I've been so wrapped up in my own self-pity, I never took time to think how Mom's leaving affected you."

The microwave chimed and he retrieved his plate of steaming food. "It's an answer to a prayer," he said, sitting next to her, "hearing you talk this way." He patted her hand. "Looks like that baby of yours has a fighting chance, after all."

After all? So there had been doubt in his mind? Not that she blamed him. The way she'd been acting all these years, who would think a girl like that could put anybody a head of her own wants and needs, let alone an innocent child?

"So is Josh good at his job?" she asked, needing to change the subject.

"The best. He plays the guitar during services, too."

"I have to admit, I'm a little surprised."

Her father took a bite. "Come on Sunday and see for yourself."

At least now she had a reason to go, other than her earlier promise to her dad. Hannah was quiet for a second then nodded. "Okay, I will."

~ THREE ~

Hannah sat in her parked car, gripping the wheel and staring at the chapel in front of her. She'd spent most of her teenage years here but it had been so long since the last time she'd stepped through the big mahogany doors. Now, as she watched the last few people trickling in, Hannah felt guilt stab at her heart. A familiar visitor now.

Realizing she had been holding her breath, she blew out a puff of air. Hannah released her hold on the wheel, hesitantly unbuckled her seat belt, and climbed out of the car. If only she were still the unscarred girl she'd been the last time she came here four years ago. As she walked into the worship hall, Hannah made a beeline for a back row seat. As she slid into one, someone tapped her on the shoulder.

"Hannah Sinclair? Is that you?"

She turned to the sound of the familiar voice and found herself face to face with Erin Beckinsal, her old high school friend. Back then Erin had been a plain Jane with flat, shoulder-length brown hair and small, almond shaped eyes. Today, she wore a hint of blush and mascara, and her once-flat stomach was now rounded. At one time Hannah envied the curves and slim waist Erin developed well before she, or any of their friends, had blossomed. Now, seeing the infant balanced on Erin's hip and the obvious result from him stretching under her shirt, Hannah became acutely aware of the danger lying ahead in the months to come.

"Erin, how are you?" She stood quickly and embraced her old friend over the back of the pew. "And who is this cutie?" Hannah tousled the little boy's hair.

Erin nodded at her little boy. "This is Cole. I have another one around here somewhere." She laughed as she glanced around.

"It's so weird to see you with a baby," Hannah admitted as she remembered the girl she used to laugh with until dawn, and cruise around in her mom's Plymouth with the windows down and radio blaring. She gave Cole a playful tug on his chubby little hand. Then, looking left and right to make sure no one stood in earshot, she leaned closer and whispered, "Last time I saw you, we were sneaking smokes in your basement."

Giggling, Erin shook her head. "A lot has changed since then." She took a step back and assessed Hannah, head to toe. "So, how are you?" Then, her grin becoming a soft smile, she added, "I've heard a few things about the exciting life you've lead, especially compared to the rest of us Linbeck folks."

She found it easier to focus on Cole's round blue eyes than meet Erin's scrutiny. "I don't have anything as exciting as a beautiful baby in my life." The angel faced child appeared happy and well cared for, proof that Erin was a doting mama. Hannah wondered if she'd be a good mother, too.

Before Erin could respond, the music started up. "Come and sit with us," Erin said, grabbing Hannah's hand. "We're right up here." She proceeded to march straight up the center aisle, all the way to the front row, where she sat beside her husband and three-year-old daughter, whose little face looked so much like Erin's that even in a crowded room, Hannah would have been able to pick her out as her friend's daughter. Hannah sat beside her. Erin nodded at the stage, then whispered, "You and Josh still friends?"

Following Erin's line of sight, Hannah saw Josh on the altar, his polished guitar hanging from a strap across his shoulders. He adjusted the microphone stand before locking his gaze to hers, a slow smile dimpling his tanned cheek. He never broke the intense eye contact, not even while strumming a chord to adjust the guitar's keys. Fingers moved deftly over the strings, and his arm muscles flexed. And then he smiled. That amazing, take-your-breath-away smile that had caused other girls to blush. This time, it was her cheeks that felt hot, making Hannah wonder why Josh had this effect on her.

Erin nudged Hannah. "Are you?"

Hannah could imagine what she must have looked like, gawking at Josh like some schoolgirl with a crush. Self-consciously she tucked her hair behind her ear and nodded. "Yeah," she said, doing her best to sound casual, "Josh and I will always be friends." And for the life of her, Hannah couldn't figure out why she longed to confess that she hoped they'd be more, soon.

"I heard he's thinking about moving to the New York church soon, to manage the missions department."

Hannah turned sharply. "New York?" She calculated the miles and hours that would put between them, and sadly wondered how their relationship could ever deepen over a distance like that.

Erin's familiar knowing smirk told Hannah she suspected more brewing than mere friendship. With a little nod, she faced forward and clapped to the music.

For the duration of worship, Hannah couldn't get her mind off what Erin said and her heart sank a little more every time *New York* echoed in her mind. She was always the one who left home, and Josh was always the one who stayed. No matter where she went, or with whom, it had been comforting knowing he would be there when she returned. Thinking that he might leave, maybe for good, made her want to cry.

Worship ended a few songs later and Hannah hoped she didn't look as distraught as she felt. Her brain fixated on what the town—and her life—would be like if Josh did leave. He had always been her go-to guy in the past—when her mom left, when a boyfriend dumped her, when a friend hurt her, or when she needed someone to laugh with. The only friend she could ever be her complete self with was Josh, and he knew it all, from her hopes and dreams to her bad habits. She was angry with herself for allowing them to lose a friendship that meant so much to them both. If only she'd shown him how much he always meant to her, then maybe he wouldn't be considering leaving.

The choir filed quietly to their seats on the altar as Josh set his guitar in its stand, then sat beside her. "You made it," he said. He leaned close, and the sweet warmth of his breath caressed her cheek.

Nodding, she said, "I promised my dad." His grin faltered, making her wish she had said something—anything—else. Josh turned toward the pulpit where her father stood, opening his timeworn Bible. It had been nearly four years since she'd heard him preach a sermon, and, as he read from Second Timothy, it made her more than a little proud.

As a young teen, Hannah never would have imagined her military father talking about the Bible and God. Yet, when he made the decision to become a pastor, he pleased the entire town by being a surprisingly good one. No one thought the retired Colonel had it in him after twenty years of military service and a wife who had up and left.

Hannah recalled her horrified reaction when he told her of his plans to make a career change. "But Dad, what will everyone think? Mom just left and—and, you're going to open a church? No one will go. You've never preached a day in your life."

He calmly responded, "It doesn't matter what everyone thinks, Hannah. It just matters that I'm doing what I've been called to do."

He definitely proved her wrong, she thought as she glanced at the large congregation.

Thirty minutes later, her father wrapped up the sermon.

Josh turned to her. "As good as you remember?"

Smiling, Hannah said, "I might come back next week."

Josh laughed as Hannah's dad approached, wearing a dark blue suit and a crisp white shirt. With his salt-and-pepper hair freshly cut, and his lean face closely shaven, he looked like he should have been in a department store ad.

"Dad, look at you." Standing, she straightened his

tie. "The last time I saw you this dressed up was at my fifth grade band concert." Normally, he sported slacks and a nice button down but she knew today he'd dressed to the nines for her.

"I'm trying something new," he teased, laughing as he stepped closer to Erin and her husband. "Good morning, guys. Glad to see you," he said, shaking their hands.

While he went about his duties, Josh turned to Hannah. "What do you have going on this afternoon?"

She looked at the ceiling, as if contemplating her packed schedule. She had been planning on getting a manicure but when Josh asked, her afternoon suddenly cleared. "Nothing big. Why?"

He shrugged. "Just wondering if you would like to go downtown with me?"

He said it slowly, as if choosing his words carefully, and Hannah wondered why. Then she remembered the time he extended a similar invitation and she ended up clinging to a rock in the middle of the river as their canoe drifted downstream while he hooted playfully from shore, camera clicking.

Hannah narrowed her eyes suspiciously. "Where downtown?"

He shrugged again and smirked. "Someplace near the mall."

"So why the secrecy? Is there a river involved?"

As if remembering that day, many summers ago, Josh laughed. "No, not a river for miles."

Intrigued, Hannah said, "Okay, but I have to warn you, I can swim now."

Josh held up one hand. "Duly noted," he said as her father made his way toward them.

"It was so good seeing you," Erin said, switching Cole from one hip to the other. "Call me sometime and we'll do lunch."

Hannah smiled, hoping her eagerness to find a friend wasn't too obvious. "Definitely. Talk to you soon, then."

"Great. Looking forward to it." Erin waved and began herding her family toward the door.

When Hannah turned around, she bumped squarely into Josh. If he hadn't reached out to steady her, she would have fallen into the aisle flat on her rear. She glanced up into green eyes that caused her breath to hitch, and lips so enticing they made her blush. A faint scent of masculine aftershave wafted up her nose as she noticed her hands, flat against his broad chest.

Blinking, Hannah took a step back and pretended to search the church for her father. "Sorry about that," she mumbled, wishing, as her cheeks blazed, that she didn't have this annoying tendency to blush at the drop of a hat.

"Ready to go?"

"Right now?" She thought he meant to take her wherever he was taking her, later, not the instant the service ended.

"Why not?" Josh said, extending a crooked elbow. She linked her arm in his and let him lead her from the church.

"You two have a good time," Hannah's dad called after them.

So her father had known Josh would invite her someplace today? *Oh, well*, Hannah thought, *if he approves, must not be a place too crazy.* "I'll try," she called back. And through narrowed eyes, she caught Josh's gaze. "Remember, no rivers," she added as a precaution. While she waited for Josh to unlock his car, Hannah noticed that Erin had parked beside him. "You remember Erin, don't you?"

He gave her an *are you kidding* look, and said, "I drop in on them now and then, and of course, I see them every Sunday." He opened the door for her and she got in, then Josh climbed in behind the wheel, started the engine, and slowly pulled away from the church.

"I can't believe she has two kids."

Josh looked out the window. "Pretty much everyone from high school is married with kids or getting married,

36

Hannah. Not many of us single people get out of here."

And even fewer who are pregnant, Hannah thought, picking at her cuticles. She wished she could tell Josh about the baby. Wished even more there was nothing to tell. Her condition was like a wall between them. Strange, since she could see something in his eyes, could feel something between them. But no matter what she felt, or wished, eventually, she'd have no choice but to tell him about the baby. Unless, of course, he left for New York before she started to show.

"You're mad at me," Hannah said, looking up at him. She saw his jaw clench as he stared through the windshield.

"I was mad at you for a long time. Now I just feel sorry for you."

Hannah's mouth dropped open. "You feel sorry for me?" She didn't know if she was more hurt or angry.

He sighed. "It's just, I mean, you seem so different since you came home. Lonely. Stand-offish." He met her eyes. "You sure aren't the carefree, crazy girl you used to be."

Talk about hitting the nail on the head, Hannah thought. The anger drained from her and left her feeling empty. "Getting out of Linbeck sounded like the road to fun and freedom," she said softly, staring out the window. "Turned out it wasn't all I thought it'd be." If her voice sounded alien in her own ears, what must it sound like to Josh? She could feel his eyes on her, and wished she could open up, let it all out. It would be a relief to share her troubles with a good friend. But it wouldn't be fair to burden Josh with her problems.

"You can't fool me, Hannah Sinclair. I can still tell when something's on your mind."

She feigned a smile. "It's nothing, Josh," she fibbed. At least, nothing he could help her with, like the time when they were ten, and lost her bike. Her dad had warned her what might happen if she took it to the river but she hadn't listened. And Josh, her faithful friend, had searched until dark until he found it floating downstream. He'd been soaked and muddy when he showed up, grinning like the Cheshire cat, and whispered into her bedroom window "It's in your shed, right where it's supposed to be." If not for the screen, she probably would have kissed him that night.

"If you don't want to talk about it—" he was saying.

"I'm sorry," Hannah interrupted, "that I didn't write, or call, or visit. Most of all," she said, facing him, "I'm sorry I hurt you." She watched him blink, then swallow, as his cheeks reddened.

"Apology accepted." There was a beat of silence.

"So," she began in a brighter voice, "what's this Erin says about you moving to New York?"

He lifted one shoulder. "Rumor has it the church in New York is looking for someone to head the missions department and my name came up. Nothing more to it right now, except some ideas being tossed around."

"I can't see you in the big city," she told him with a shake of her head. "No way."

There was no mistaking the way he tightened his grip on the steering wheel. "It's just ideas," he said, his voice as tight as his fingers. "I'll know more at the end of the year."

Josh's reaction to her comment was evidence of how they'd grown apart over the years. Hannah looked out the window again. Squinting, she wrinkled her nose. "Where are we?"

One corner of his mouth lifted in a wry grin as he turned into a torn-up parking lot surrounded by weeds. "Like I said, we're near the mall."

From her vantage point, Hannah could see the road signs. "We're in Allen County..." she stated slowly, and as they parked, she spied a crooked sign hanging over a rickety doorway. "...at the homeless shelter."

Josh unbuckled his seat belt and climbed out of the car. Hannah quickly followed.

"If you'd told me we were coming here, I would have

changed my clothes." She smoothed the front of her dress. "How will it look, me going in there like this, and them, barely able to clothe themselves?" she said, mostly to herself.

"I didn't tell you, because I wanted to surprise you." Josh pressed a palm to her lower back and led her through a side door.

Surprise, indeed. Not what she had been expecting but found herself happy that Josh was opening his new life up to her, a world that she missed for four years.
"Are we going to preach to them?" Hannah asked in a low voice, suddenly panicking that she wouldn't be able to remember a scripture.

Josh chuckled as they made their way down a long, chipped linoleum floor. "No, no. Nothing like that. We're going to serve them lunch. I promise, you'll feel good about it later." Josh opened a splintered wooden door that housed a greasy window.

The smell and heat of the kitchen immediately hit Hannah in the face, causing her stomach to churn. The room was small, with open tubs of soup, potatoes, and meat floating in gravy, lining the stainless countertops. Three men in white aprons filled metal serving dishes, while several women plopped it onto Styrofoam plates. A line of tired, tattered people waited for their share of the food. Hannah felt another wave of nausea hit her.

"Are you all right?" Josh asked, looking concerned. "You look like you don't feel so hot."

With one hand over her mouth, she spun on her heel and raced down the hall, going back the way they'd come. She'd barely made it out the door before her breakfast came up. Bent over and heaving, Hannah became aware of Josh standing behind her. Not knowing if she was more horrified to be puking outside a homeless shelter or that Josh was there to witness it, Hannah wished she were at home to bury herself under a mound of blankets and hide from the world.

Josh wrapped an arm around her and bent near her face. "Good grief, Baby, are you okay?"

Nodding weakly, Hannah rooted in her purse for a tissue and, straightening, wiped her face. She leaned against the crumbling brick wall, and closed her eyes to the bright hot sunlight beating down on them.

"I'm sorry, Hannah. I'd never have insisted you come if I knew you were sick." Josh ran a hand through his hair. "Why didn't you tell me you didn't feel well?"

"Breakfast didn't agree with me today, I guess." She laid a hand on her stomach. "I'm fine, now."

Josh pressed a palm to her forehead. "You're not feverish, at least. Still," he said, eyes narrowed as he studied her face. "C'mon," he said, digging in his pockets for his keys, "let's get you home."

Humiliated, Hannah stared at the ground and grew angrier still at her unborn baby. *You're ruining everything,* she mentally told it. *Nothing has been the same since I learned about you.* Almost instantly, regret rose inside her. Hannah knew in her heart the baby wasn't to blame for the way her world had changed. Everything wrong with her life was her own fault. Dumb decisions, immaturity, self-centeredness... everything bad she'd ever done had caught up with her all at the same time. Things were going to have to change if she hoped to regain any sort of control over things.

"No," Hannah said emphatically. "I'm not sick."

Josh's brows drew together in a concerned frown. "Your recent actions would say otherwise." He felt her forehead again. "You're definitely not warm but you're still looking a little under the weather."

Exasperated, Hannah grabbed his wrist. "I appreciate your concern, really I do, but I'm okay now." She attempted a shaky smile. "Don't you think I'm the best judge of what I'm capable of?"

"All right. But we can leave any time you want," he said, holding the door open for her.

Hannah marched into the kitchen and grabbed an apron, sliding it over her head as another wave of people entered the doors for lunch.

"Let me introduce you to a couple of the other volunteers," Josh said, waving to get their attention. One by one, they approached, smiling and reaching for her hand as he introduced them. "This is Jerry, the cook. Sherry and her husband, Cade. Here's Jim and his daughter, Tonya, and Steve, he serving community service time so he won't go back to prison."

Hannah tried, and failed, to hide the tiny gasp that popped from her mouth. Soon, all the volunteers joined Steve in a round of laughter.

"Just kidding," Josh laughed, shaking his head. "You should've seen your face."

Hannah knew she was blushing. Again. "You had me there for a minute," she said to Josh. And to the others, she added, "That's only because I figured Steve was one of Josh's ex-con pals."

Laughter echoed around the stainless and ceramic kitchen. Still chuckling, everyone manned their stations and served the quickly growing line of hungry homeless. Hannah had been assigned to dole out mashed potatoes and gravy, and as each person shuffled by, plate extended, her heart ached. She'd seen poor people before, in nearly every European country. But never had she been up close to them like now. Their ratty clothes, grimy skin, and yellow teeth only echoed the haunted despair in their sad, dull eyes. Still, they smiled and uttered heartfelt thanks as she mounded their plates with a hefty portion of potatoes.

After a few minutes, Hannah glanced at Josh, spooning soup into their bowls while making small talk about the weather and the latest sports scores. She admired him so much in that moment, and said a silent prayer that when her "changing" was complete, she'd share his concern for others and the ease with which he showed them that he cared. More than anything, she hoped that someday, she'd feel as comfortable in her own skin as he seemed to be in his.

Josh chose that moment to look up and sent a warm, genuine smile her way. She returned it, and for the first time in a long, long time, felt it, right to her core.

"Ahem," said the elderly woman in front of her.

"Sorry," Hannah said, grinning sheepishly.

The woman gave a gap-toothed grin and shook her plate. "All's I want is some spuds, girlie, with plenty of that gravy. When I'm gone, you can gaze at that good-lookin' fella all day long if you want."

Giggling to herself, Hannah filled the woman's request. A sense of peace settled over her as the next fellow in line stepped up to her station. Never in her life had she gone hungry. In fact, she'd have been hard-pressed to think of the last time her stomach even growled between meals. Blinking back hot tears, she dropped a scoop of potatoes onto his plate, realizing how much she had to be thankful for, and how long it had been since she'd admitted it. It wasn't going to be easy—finding a job, a place to live, being a loving, single parent—but something told her she could do it.

By late afternoon, Hannah's feet ached, her back hurt, and the experience had caused a permanent nauseous throb in her stomach. They finished putting leftovers into the refrigerators, and after the final counter was wiped down, said their goodbyes and retreated down the hallway. Hannah took a huge gulp of fresh air when she stepped outside. How strange it seemed to feel no need whatever to speak. The comfortable silence between them grew as she climbed into Josh's car.

"Oh," she sighed. "It's good to get off my feet."
In place of a reply, Josh merely looked at her. Hannah returned his gaze, lost in deep, green eyes. A long moment passed until she smiled. "What..."

He draped an arm over the back of the seat. "You never cease to amaze me, Baby Sinclair."

"Oh?"

"You were sick as a dog the entire time but you fed those people anyway. You didn't let them so much as guess that it was a struggle." He wrapped a tendril of her hair around his forefinger. "I'm proud of you."

His thumb traced the contours of her cheek, and for a moment, it looked as if he might kiss her. Instead, he winked, then turned and revved up the engine.

"It wasn't nearly as bad as I thought it would be," she confessed. "I felt... it felt good." Hannah laughed a bit. "Other than the getting sick part, of course."

For the rest of the drive, they chatted companionably about the shelter and its volunteers. For Hannah, the trip ended way too soon.

"Talk to you soon?" she asked, when Josh turned the car into her driveway.

"You bet."

When she slid from the front seat, he reached across and grabbed her hand. "Hey," he gave it a gentle squeeze. "The carnival is in town this week. Maybe... maybe we could go together or something."

Hannah returned the squeeze. "Ah, the annual Fun Fest." Nodding, she giggled. "Good times. I'd love to go... together or something. So, would that make it a real-live date?"

Josh's grin broadened. "Yeah," he said with slight hesitation, "I guess it would."

"Let me know what night's best for you, so I can check my oh-so-packed calendar," she teased. And with a final glance, Hannah climbed out of the car. Her heart ached as she watched him drive away, and though she doubted he could see it, she waved goodbye.

Heading up the walk, her mind raced. *Why had Josh invited her to the fair in such a tentative way? And why, had his answer about it being a real date been so evasive? And when are you going to tell him about the baby?*

That question alone was enough to erase the smile

from her face and the good mood she'd been in. When she walked through the door, her dad sat in the living room, peering over the newspaper at her.

"Ah, you're back." He gave the paper a shake and laid it in his lap. "So, how'd it go?"

She could tell by his self-satisfied grin that he'd been in on the scheme to get her to the shelter. "You traitor. You were in on it with Josh, weren't you?" She kidded him.

He grinned. "It was Josh's idea. So, how'd it go?"

Hannah flopped into an exhausted heap on the couch. "Had my first real bout with morning sickness. Aside from that, it was great."

Concern lined his face and he leaned forward. "You got sick?"

She nodded. "Nothing huge. I was better by the time lunch was served."

"I'm proud of you," he said from behind the newspaper.

Hannah had seen the truth of his words glittering in his gray eyes, and it made her heart swell with love. "Josh wants to take me to *Fun Fest* one night this week." She leaned on the sofa arm and tucked her legs beneath her and waited.

As expected, her dad peeked over the paper, eyeglasses low on his nose. "An official date?" She hadn't expected the note of disapproval in his voice, or the slight frown on his face. No doubt he was worried about Josh, getting too involved with his wayward, pregnant-and-unmarried daughter. Not that she blamed him, exactly. Still, it hurt.

"No. Not a date," she said, remembering Josh's tone when she'd asked the same question. "Just two friends hanging out like we used to."

One brow lifted. "Have you told him yet that you're pregnant?"

Years of irresponsibility and selfishness were cause

for his attitude. She could hardly blame him for wondering about her motives. Staring at her hands, Hannah sighed. "Not yet. But I will."

"You'd better not wait too long. That boy has always had a thing for you. You don't want to break his heart a second time."

A second time? Had she been so self-involved that she hadn't even noticed how Josh felt about her, or about her leaving? And staying gone so long without a word? Hannah's heart ached. She had a lot to make up for. "I'll tell him. Soon. I promise."

Hannah felt the stirrings of romance between her and Josh, so it wasn't a far reach to believe he'd felt that way for a long time, and kept his feelings to himself. She'd make it up to him for the past hurts she'd caused him by ensuring he'd never be hurt by her again.

~ FOUR ~

Hannah sipped on her water while anxiously staring out the diner's window. Around her, the smell of eggs and bacon heavily scented the air, making her stomach growl in empty anticipation. The place was busier than she would have imagined for a Tuesday morning. Two moms sat in a booth corralling their five young children while they tried unconvincingly to get them to eat. A couple of men in suits shared an animated conversation from the center of the diner, while an elderly couple sat quietly in front of the windows, gazing mildly out at the passersby as they sipped their coffee.

Hannah glanced around the diner, surprised to not see one familiar face. Since when had this town grown to the point that there were strangers among them? The diner itself hadn't even been here when she lived in Linbeck. Things at home, she sadly realized, had kept going in spite of her absence. As a little girl she'd always thought that time stood still while she was away. In her mind, Josh would always be there, her mom wouldn't age a bit even after years of desertion, and Linbeck would be the same little town she'd always known. Instead, everything had aged and grown. The world had continued racing through life as if change couldn't happen fast enough. And here she was, definitely not the same girl she used to be.

Erin came hurrying across Main Street, looking flustered as she redistributed the weight of her hefty handbag to the other shoulder. Hannah waved enthusiastically through the window. Erin spotted her and returned the gesture with a bright smile as she whipped the diner's door open.

Out of breath, she slid into the booth. "Sorry I'm late! The kids were getting into everything and my mom needed help with the baby..." she waved her hand in the air, cutting her explanation short. "Anyway, I'm here. It's

46

good to see you. I was so happy when you called yesterday."

Hannah smiled at her friend. "It's been too long
since we've hung out. I've missed you."

The waiter approached. "You ladies want to see a
menu?"

"Yes, thanks," Erin told him. "I'm so hungry I could
eat everything in here."

"Me too," Hannah agreed, refraining from comment-
ing about why she'd been so hungry lately.

Quickly scanning the selection, they placed their orders before the waiter could escape. When he left, Erin
turned her attention back to Hannah.
"You look great, Hannah. College suits you," she said ear-
nestly. "So what's it like coming back home after all these
years?"

Hannah ignored the compliment, wanting to avoid
thoughts about college altogether. If only Erin knew... but
that was part of the reason Hannah called her. She needed
a friend, someone to talk to about this. Someone other
than her father, and someone who would only want to give
her advice and encouragement. While she needed that at
times, she was also craving someone to give it to her how it
was, harsh reality and all. The ups and downs of pregnancy,
what she'd be going through in the months ahead, the
pluses and the minuses. Erin had been there and done that
already, and she would understand without judgment. And
quite frankly, Hannah needed a good girlfriend to confide
in.

"It's..." Hannah thought about it a moment. "Not
what I expected. I mean, things have changed so much in
four years. There's new restaurants, new stores, unfamiliar
people. I believed Linbeck would always be the same."

Erin nodded, taking a sip of her coffee. "A lot of
people from Springfield have been coming here to get away
from the high taxes and housing costs. Good for them, not
so much for us," she admitted. "So have you run into any-

one from high school?"

"Other than you and Josh, no. It's crazy. Back then you couldn't go anywhere without seeing someone you knew."

Erin leaned forward a little, her eyes sparkling with curiosity. "Speaking of Josh, how's it been seeing him again?"

Trying to look nonchalant, Hannah shrugged. "Good. Real good." She stole a quick glance at Erin, who looked inquisitively at her. She sighed. "Honestly, I don't know. He was mad at me for barely talking to him for four years and, well, who could blame him? We were best friends. I shouldn't have been so rude to not even think of him."

"Josh knows you better than anyone. He'll come around," Erin said.

"He seemed more his old self on Sunday. Maybe he needed to hear an apology." She took a drink of water.

Erin laughed and waved a hand through the air. "Oh please, girl. He would have forgiven you no matter what. The man's always been crazy about you."

Hannah suddenly choked on her water and launched into a coughing fit. That was the second time she'd heard mention of Josh's feelings for her. Had she been that blind? She managed to get control of her sputtering while Erin looked on in amusement.

Their food arrived then, the steaming aroma enough to silence them both for a few seconds while they claimed their silverware and dug in.

"Am I missing something here?" Hannah asked around a mouthful of eggs. "My dad and you have both said something about Josh 'being crazy' about me." She stabbed the air with her fork.

Erin shrugged and shuffled her hash browns around. "Everyone we grew up with thought so. He's never come out and said it, but it's always been pretty obvious. Why do you think a hottie like him is still single? He knew you'd come back one day," she said with a wink.

"He's dated in the last four years, hasn't he?" Hannah asked, finding it hard to believe that she didn't have a clue about Josh's life anymore.

"Sure. He's dated plenty, but no one was ever around longer than a couple months. He has high expectations," Erin told her, seemingly enjoying the conversation. "Why? You interested?" she teased.

Nearly choking again, Hannah hid behind her food as she took another bite. *Maybe I am interested*, she thought. *But what's the point? I'm not ready for another relationship*. And the thought of one with Josh was too much for her to wrap her brain around at the moment. Besides, she was pretty sure Josh wasn't ready for a relationship with his old best friend that was now single and pregnant.

"Hannah?" Erin frowned at her, interrupting her thoughts. "You look troubled. You okay?"

She forgot how well her old friends knew her. Never good at hiding her feelings, Hannah knew Erin could sense she wasn't getting the whole story. Swallowing, she put her fork down and stared hard at the plate of still-steaming food.

"Oh Erin," Hannah began, but already, the tears were coming. "I'm..."

"Let me guess... pregnant?" Erin finished for her, immediately reaching forward and covering Hannah's hand with her own.

Hannah glanced up sharply, wondering if it were that obvious. "How'd you know?"

Erin patted her sympathetically. "There are only a few things a young woman can get that sad about. And number one when you're single is getting pregnant."

Managing a small laugh, Hannah quickly wiped the tears away. "What's number two?"

"Watching the man she loves get married to someone else."

"I don't know which one would be worse," Hannah joked. "I'm sorry, I shouldn't burden you with my problems."

Looking offended, Erin playfully swatted her. "Are you kidding? It may have been four years, but I'm still your second right-hand man."

"Second?"

"Next to Josh, of course. That's the way it always was and always will be. Josh first, everyone else second."

"If what you say is true about Josh liking me, I doubt he'll continue being my 'right-hand man.' I've put him through enough and this will probably be the clincher."

"So you haven't told him, I gather?" Erin resumed eating.

Hannah shook her head and pushed her plate aside, no longer hungry. "I'm so ashamed of it. He's this success-ful pastor and missionary and I'm knocked up by some loser ex-boyfriend."

"Honey, you're not a loser. You're human. You made a mistake, but it's not the end of the world. And Josh will probably surprise you. He's a good man and would never judge you like that."

"Maybe you're right. I can't bring myself to disap-point him anymore than I already have."

Erin raised her brow. "You shouldn't worry so much about Josh. There are plenty of other things that need your attention. Like that baby."

"Right again." Hannah laughed. "I knew you'd be the right person to talk to."

"Look hon, I'm always here for you, you know that. So..." She moved her plate away and leaned forward again, giving Hannah her undivided attention. "Who's the guy?"

Hannah took a deep breath, finding it harder than she thought to bring up her ex. "His name is Ben. We dated on and off for about three years. Right before graduation, I caught him with my roommate."

Erin grimaced. "Ouch. Does he know about the ba-by?"

"I think he has a pretty good idea. I haven't been

able to bring myself to call him yet."

"So this has all been pretty recent?"

Hannah nodded glumly. "A couple of weeks ago." They lapsed into silence, the clinks of plates and chatter filling the air.

"Who needs him anyway? You're back home, safe and sound now."

"I'm relieved to be back," Hannah admitted. "Sometimes you just need what only your hometown can offer."

"Here, here. You know what else you need?"

Hannah looked up at her friend. "What's that?"

"You need to do a little shopping with an old friend. C'mon." She slapped a twenty on the table and gathered her purse.

"Erin, I'm not letting you buy breakfast. I called you, so I've got it." Hannah rummaged through her purse, but Erin had already gotten to her feet.

"No, no. I insist. Let's go, dear. My mom only has so much in her before she'll be blowing up my cell phone begging me to come home."

Hannah sighed and slid from the booth. "Fine. But I've got it next time."

Erin giggled and looped her arm through Hannah's. "Next time it is, then. How about Thursday?"

"Deal." Hannah followed her friend out the doors into the early afternoon sunlight.

~ * ~

"I'm coming, I'm coming," Hannah sang to her reflection as she hurriedly applied lip-gloss. Smacking her lips, she tossed the tube into her dresser drawer, made one last check of her hair and eyes, then took a deep breath and raced down the stairs to meet Josh.

He'd made himself comfortable on the living room couch. Time stood still for an instant as she watched him, chatting with her dad, whose 'do what's best for Josh' lecture had made her late. Much as she hated to admit it, her father had been right to worry that her problems would become Josh's, possibly ruining his entire life, and she wanted that even less than her father did.

Straightening her shoulders, Hannah plastered a grin on her face and breezed into the room, doing her best to avoid her dad's disapproving stare. He didn't know it yet, but she intended to keep her promise. Tonight, she'd tell Josh about the baby and put an end to their apparently blossoming relationship.

"Ready," she said, forcing a note of joy into her voice.

Standing, Josh smiled. "You sure? The carnival doesn't close until midnight. We still have time."

"Ha, ha," she said, gathering her purse and keys.

Josh stood on the front porch, holding the door. It was when he glanced at a passing car that Hannah caught sight of another warning look from her dad. "Don't worry, Dad," she said quietly, stepping outside. "I intend to keep my promise."

"I'll have her back by curfew, Michael." Josh laughed and Hannah nearly shoved him off the porch.

"You'd better," her father returned, "I know where you live."

They made their way down the front walk. Hannah couldn't help thinking how ironic it was that Josh wanted to protect her chastity, and her dad had gone along with it, knowing full well it was way too late for that.

Josh held the car door, and she slid into the passenger seat "I meant to tell you earlier," an adorable half-smile brightening his handsome face, "you look great."

Hannah smiled, feeling her worries dissolve. "Thanks. So do you," she said, feeling suddenly shy.

"Ready to rock-and-roll?" Josh backed out of the drive.

Catching onto his playful mood, Hannah said, "Ready as ever."

"Then a great time we shall have." Josh cast her his lopsided grin and tuned the radio station to a country channel.

Fishin' in the Dark, by Nitty Gritty Dirt Band suddenly burst through the speakers. Simultaneously, they looked
at one another and laughed.

"Been a while since I've heard this." Hannah jumped
in right on chorus, the song having always been their favorite for as long as she could remember.

But as they sang the familiar lyrics together and she
saw Josh's warm gaze meet her own, Hannah found her
thoughts drifting. She couldn't ignore the dread she felt at
having to tell him about the baby. If not for her pregnancy,
she could only imagine where this relationship would go.
And yet, despite the enormity of her mistake, she knew her
options were limited.

If she hadn't been a God-fearing girl, raised by her
Christian dad, how easy it would have been to erase the
problem, like an arithmetic mistake. But even though she'd
grown apart from her town, her church, even her father,
Hannah never gave more than a passing thought to the idea
of abortion. She'd done a dumb thing, getting involved with
Ben, but the baby shouldn't have to pay for her mistakes.
That meant this baby was coming, one way or another.
With, or without, Josh.

"Look," Josh said, interrupting her reverie, "you can
see the glow of carnival lights from here."

Hannah looked through the windshield. From the
country road, the carnival lights illuminated the inky
blackness in a cloud of bright, blinking lights. The summer
air smelled of fresh cut grass and perfumed flowers, the
wind cutting sharply through the open windows.

"Beautiful night," she said distractedly.

He grabbed her hand. "Yep, beautiful."

She was tempted to pull away. To ask him to take
her home. To confess her sins and get that nasty matter
over with. Yet she couldn't bring herself to hurt him. The
glow on his face told her how happy he was to be there
with her, and she didn't want to ruin that just yet. Josh

was a prize, in every imaginable way. Tall, handsome, and hardworking, he'd make any young woman a wonderful husband. And she'd seen him with the kids at church. He'd be a great father, too.

"So, why aren't you married, like every other guy we graduated with?" Hannah asked.

Josh only shrugged. "I've been busy."

That inspired a tiny chuckle. "Busy? For four years?" Another giggle, and then, "Your problem is, you're too picky. Always have been."

Raising his brow, he gazed into her eyes. "I haven't lived like a monk, you know. I've dated. I even took Emma Baines out a couple times."

Her archenemy since the second grade? "No way!"

Emma had been in love with Josh since kindergarten, and hated Hannah for no reason other than she was Josh's friend. She'd told Hannah in high school that she didn't be-lieve for a minute their relationship was strictly platonic, and that once Josh saw what she was willing to do—for oth-er guys—he'd drop Hannah in a second. It hadn't worked, at least, not back then. Had Emma's plan been more suc-cessful recently? Hannah's stomach twisted with unex-pected jealously.

Josh nodded. "Ran into her at the grocery store one day, got to talking." He waved the sentence away. "Wasn't a big deal."

"Hmm." Hannah grinned. "I'd bet my life savings she followed you there. If I had a life savings."

Chuckling, Josh nodded. "Probably."

"So what happened?"

Hannah noticed a blush creeping slowly into his cheeks as he kept his eyes straight ahead, on the road. "Took her to dinner couple times, that's all."

"Ahhh, I see. And where did you take her, exactly?"

Josh turned into the fairgrounds and waited as some guy with a flashlight directed the cars ahead of him to parking spaces. When he didn't respond, Hannah's heart sank.

"Don't tell me you took her to Sandy's," she said, attempting and failing to keep the hurt from her voice.

He cleared his throat and looked away. Sandy's had always been their place. It was the scene of three years of prom dinners, and every special occasion before, between, and after. Neither had ever gone there without the other in all their years of friendship.

Josh had been picky, but so had Hannah. She couldn't even begin to count the number of hours they'd logged, hammering on this guy or that girl, and all the reasons not to date them. So they'd attended nearly every high school function together, telling one another it was safe and smart to do things like that with a trusted friend. *"A friend won't hurt you," he'd said once.*

But she had hurt him, deeply.

"Yeah," Josh said at last. "I took her there, but only once." He heaved a heavy sigh. "That was the night I realized Emma and I had absolutely nothing in common."

A moment of silence hung heavy between them as Hannah struggled to swallow her unjust disappointment. What right did she have to be jealous? Still, she couldn't shake the feeling.

"You're a great guy, Josh. You deserve someone special. Someone who can make you happy."

Josh's gaze held hers. She detected regret, but also something else. "You're right."

Hannah's breath caught in her throat, and she swallowed at the intensity of his stare. Warning signals were going off in her mind as she realized where this was leading.

"Whoa," she said, forcing a note of merriment into her voice in an attempt to steer the conversation elsewhere. "Let's put that on the calendar." She finger-wrote in the air, "Josh says I'm right. That's a first!"

Josh grinned with a shake of his head. It was their turn to park, and once he turned off the ignition, he turned slightly in the seat, looking serious again. He opened his mouth to say something, then thought better of it and faced forward again. "That line is pretty long," he said quietly, opening his car door.

Hannah sat in silence, staring as he walked around the front of the car to open her door. The scent of popcorn, cotton candy, and deep-fried *Twinkies* floated on the gentle breeze, and squeals of laughter echoed above the grinding and clanking of the ancient rides.

"Nothing's changed," she said, stepping into the ankle-deep grass.

"Never does," he agreed, grabbing her hand and slamming the passenger door. "Same stuff, different year," he added. "So where do you want to start, the *Twister*?"

It pleased her to know he remembered the ride had been one of their favorites. "Of course." She leaned into him.

After buying a long rope of tickets, they climbed into the big red bucket seats. The operator made his rounds, lowering the lap bars until they all locked into place.

"Let's hope we don't have a repeat of what happened at the shelter." Josh patted her thigh. "Sure you're up for this?"

Before she answered, the ride kicked into gear and they began slowly spinning. "Guess we'll soon find out," she joked, gripping the bar with all her might.

As kids, the *Twister* would get them both laughing until their stomachs cramped and they could barely sit up straight. And when it ended, they'd circle round, right back through the gate, and into another seat. If they were lucky, they'd stay seated as the ride started again.

Tonight, things were different. Every time Josh slid into her, Hannah felt an electric shock emanate through her. With every brush of his hand or bump of his knee, the warmth of his skin would cause the breath to catch in her throat, and she'd wait for the next swirl that would slide them into one another again.

When the ride slowed to a stop, Hannah tried to calm her fluttering heart and hide her blushing cheeks.

"Want another go at it?" he asked after the operator raised the lap bar.

"No thanks," she said, standing. "I'm not ten years old anymore." Then he pressed a palm to the small of her back to help her from the platform, and she sighed, feeling like a teenager with a crush on the high school quarterback.

He kept his hand there as they walked down the mid- way, and all the while, Hannah knew she must tamp down these feelings, and fast. It wasn't fair to Josh to lead him on. Wouldn't be fair to her, either. She was lonely and vulnerable, Hannah knew, and until her life made more sense, she shouldn't even consider another relationship. *Far better to end things now, before anything more develops between us.*

"You all right?" Josh was looking at her. "You're awfully quiet."

"I'm just... I was... hey, look," she said, pointing to change the subject. "Funnel cakes!"

"Anything to please my lady."

His lady? Much as it pleased her to hear those words, it hurt, because she and Josh could never be a couple. And the ugly fact was, after tonight, it was doubtful they'd even be friends.

She saved a picnic table while he bought two funnel cakes. When he sat on the bench opposite her, she took the one he offered her and fingered it, then tore a piece off and slid it into her mouth. "So, tell me about your missions."

He pulled off a piece of fried dough. "What do you want to know?"

Hannah looked up for a second, contemplating. "Do you like the work?"

"Love it," Josh said with a definitive nod.

He hadn't hesitated before answering, and the light

in his eyes was further proof how much he enjoyed it. "Where has the work taken you?"

"Guatemala, Costa Rica, Belize, Mexico...."

"Wow," Hannah said. "How exciting, traveling to all those places. What're they like?"

"Poor. Real poor. Lots of little villages where people live in crude huts without fresh water. A lot of them are seriously ill because they bathe in the same water they use as a bathroom. The kids are illiterate, neglected, starving." He sighed. "It's sad." Then, brightening a bit, he added, "But they're hungry for the truth, for a God that loves them. They know happiness isn't just about their physical needs, it's about their spiritual hunger and thirst, too." He shrugged. "So, we supply them with food and medicine, and teach them about the Bible, God's salvation, and baptism."

Hannah thought about it for a second. "Remember in middle school when I volunteered at the Humane Society for the summer?" Josh nodded, looking amused. "Well, I did it because I wanted to help those poor animals that were starving, homeless, and abused. But every day when I left, I felt horrible, because I was helpless to do more. And you're dealing with children and hard-working people who must feel awful they can't do more for their kids." She sighed. "How do you do it, Josh? How do you handle seeing all that misery, knowing there's only so much you can do?"

Josh thought for a second, looking pleased at her insight. "If I can make even a small difference in one person's life, I'm happy because it's proof I'm doing something useful with my own life."

He was a remarkable man. She wondered if Josh knew how remarkable he was. Hannah took another bite of the cake. "Wow. Deep stuff," she said to lighten the conversation.

Laughing, he said, "So, why did you feel you needed to travel the world, repel from mountains, and dive with the sharks to be happy?"

She traced a knothole on the picnic table. "I think you already know the answer to that question."

He shook his head. "No, I don't. I never did understand it."

Hannah didn't believe for a minute that he had no idea why she'd left. They'd spent hours, after all, talking about the way her mom had deserted her and her dad. Dozens of times, she'd confessed how it made her feel, knowing her own mother cared so little about her, and how, someday, she intended to try and find the woman, tell her to her face what a thoughtless, mean thing she'd done, running away from home like a spoiled child.

It dawned on Hannah, suddenly, that leaving Linbeck when she did was tantamount to walking in her mother's shoes. She could pretend the trips and treks were some sort of mother quest, but in her heart, Hannah finally understood she was running away, too. But fleeing a hurtful past hadn't brought her mother back, nor had it made her feel better about the fact that she meant so little to the woman.

Josh knew, and understood, and that's why he'd always had such a problem with the way she'd left town. She looked at him then, and saw in his green eyes all the forgiveness she'd been searching for.

Hannah looked down, away from Josh's intense stare. Shame burned in her cheeks. "There isn't a good excuse for what I did. Everything here reminded me of my mom. I guess in my little-girl head, I thought if I left town, I could leave all that hurt and resentment behind."

Josh was quiet for a second. "Your dad mentioned that she looked you up."

Even the memory of it stirred up anger. "The only time I saw her was when she needed money or a place to crash."

Softly, Josh asked, "You want some advice?" Leaning close, he laid both hands on her shoulders, forcing her to look up at him. "Stop running, Baby. There's nowhere else

59

to go."

Hannah searched his face, seeing clearly now that Josh wasn't just the best friend she'd grown up with. He was more. So much more. It didn't matter if he wanted her, flaws and all, or that she wanted him. Because of the mess she'd made of her life, she couldn't have him.

She smiled up at him, trying to mask the regret welling inside her. To distract from the threat of tears she felt brewing, Hannah pointed. "Bet I can beat you at a game of darts."

Josh watched her, his brow raised. Then he gave her a short nod, accepting the change of subject. "You're on."

They walked over to a booth lined with a pegboard lined with balloons. "*Pop one and win a prize*," Hannah read the dingy sign hanging from the awning. "What do you want me to win for you?" She grinned as the attendant handed her four darts.

Snorting good-naturedly, Josh leaned against the tent pole. "You choose... *if* you win," he taunted her.

Hannah's first dart landed between two balloons. Each dart after followed suit and hit the first one dead on, except the last one. It popped a balloon, then bounced off the board onto the floor. Delighted, Hannah did a little dance of triumph and chose a stuffed yellow and black caterpillar. "For you," she said, handing it to Josh.

"Thanks," he said, grinning. "You hold onto it for a minute and watch while a master does his magic." Picking up his darts, he added, "Step aside, little lady."

It was Hannah's turn to lean and watch as Josh took aim, threw his darts, and missed all four times.

When he faced her, she handed him the caterpillar. "Seems the master is a bit rusty," she said, giggling.

Josh huffed and said, "How about we ride the Ferris Wheel and then we get out of here?"

Hannah checked her watch. Only ten o'clock. "Where are we going?" She wasn't looking forward to leaving the fair. That meant she'd have to tell him and ruin this perfect evening, and possibly their friendship. The thought sent her stomach rolling.

He winked, casually slinging his arm around her shoulders. "You'll see."

"Another surprise." She, glanced at him suspiciously. She'd trusted him all her life, and saw no reason to stop now. "I guess I'm in your capable hands, then."

After a short wait in line, they climbed into a wobbly seat. Soon, they were carried high into the air, far above the carnival and the crowds, where everything seemed smaller, even the noisy din of equipment and the riders' squeals of glee.

Josh had slung an arm over the seat back, his finger-tips grazing her hair. Hannah tried to ignore the thrill that went through her at his touch. *A life with Josh could have been good*, she thought. Hannah sighed contentedly as he pulled her close to him. But she couldn't lead him on. She had to keep a careful, deliberate distance from him - phys-ically and emotionally - for both their sakes. So she straightened and pretended to gaze over the rail, wishing such a small thing as being in his arms wasn't such a wrong thing.

"I'm glad you're back," Josh said quietly, oblivious to her attempts at putting distance between them.

Hannah nodded. Regardless of everything, she was glad, too.

Josh pointed at different rides, at the dim lights of the city, off in the distance, and made note of the full moon.

"It looks a little like one of those Chinese lanterns," Hannah said, gazing dreamily at it clinging to its place in the sky. "Don't you think?"

When he didn't respond, she turned toward him, and before she knew what was happening, Josh's lips pressed softly against hers. For a moment, Hannah didn't know what to do, except to kiss him back. She leaned into him, surprised at the intense jolt of heat that slid through her.

But just as soon as it began, Hannah willed herself to try to pull away.

"Josh," she managed to say against his lips.

Reading her struggling thoughts before she could say them, Josh pulled back. Her lips still hot from his, the cool breeze that blew between them was disconcerting. Hannah saw that Josh's eyes were dark with longing, and watched with dismay as he ran a hand through his hair, a gesture he'd always done when he was upset.

"Sorry," he mumbled. "I don't know what came over me."

"Don't apologize," Hannah said. *I'm the one who's sorry*, she thought sadly.

The ride finally stopped and they slowly walked back to his car. *Tell him now,* she thought. *Tell him.* But the words wouldn't come. They lodged in her throat and stubbornly remained hidden inside. "So where's this mystery place you said you were going to take me?" she asked instead.

Josh fished the keys from his pocket and unlocked the car door, then stepped aside as Hannah got in. "If we go, we might break curfew," he teased.

"Can you believe I have a curfew and I'm twenty-three years old?" Laughing, she added, "And you still haven't answered the question."

Josh winked. "You'll see."

He steered back onto the highway, and as they headed north, he led the conversation into pleasant small talk.

"Hey, this is starting to look familiar," Hannah said after a while, looking around.

The airport had been their refuge in high school. When life was going wrong, they would drive there to watch the planes and get away for a while. Their last visit, she recalled, had been right after the SAT's, when both felt anxious over how they'd done. And as always, one reassured the other.

On the outskirts of town, Josh parked near a fence that girded an empty, stretching field. In the distance, the blinking lights of the airport interrupted the darkness. He turned off the car and they sat silently, staring out the windshield for a second. Then he turned and looked at her. "It's been a long time since we've been here." He opened the door.

Hannah followed him into dark, fresh summer air, where nothing moved but a breeze. Not a house in sight, no crickets chirping, no cars passing by. The place was eerily quiet, just as she remembered.

Josh slid onto the hood of his car and leaned against the windshield, lacing the fingertips of both hands behind his head. He looked at her. "What are you waiting for?" He pointed at the jet-black sky. "I think I hear one."

In the distance, the rumble of an engine grew louder, until the earth beneath her feet began to quake. As instructed, she climbed onto the car and stretched out beside him as the deafening roar vibrated through them. And then a gigantic jet screamed toward the nearest runway. Hands over her ears, Hannah watched as the blinking, lighted belly of the plane slid by overhead, landing with a thud as the engine whined and the brakes screeched in protest. It taxied into the distance, turning toward the gate, and all was silent again.

Hannah crossed her arms over her chest, looking at stars that twinkled above them. Soon, another plane approached, this time from the south, growing louder and louder until, once again, she was forced to plug her ears.

Once it made its way to the building, Josh sat up. "I almost forgot," he said, sliding off the hood.

Hannah rolled onto her side, peering through the windshield to see him rummaging in the glove box. He withdrew a small black box, and beside her once more, he handed it to her.

Hesitantly, Hannah accepted it on an open palm. "What's the occasion?" She gripped it tightly.

63

"Welcome home," Josh said with an eager smile. "Open it, will ya!"

A strange mix of elation and excitement swirled in her head as she lifted the cover. Inside, on a pillow of white satin, lay a small, silver cross with a single diamond in its center. "Oh, Josh," she said, taking it from the box. It dangled on a sparkling silver chain, reflecting both moonlight and starlight. "It's beautiful." She met his eyes, doing her best to blink back stinging tears. Her heart ached with gratitude and sadness. "You shouldn't have, but I love it," she said, smiling at him.

He even remembered that she preferred dainty jewelry to big, clunky stuff. Instinct made her lean close to hug him, and in the instant before reality set in, reminding her she had a confession to make soon, Hannah inhaled the masculine scent of his cologne, reveled in the warmth of his skin. "Thank you," she said, handing the necklace to Josh. "Will you put it on me?"

She swept her hair up in one hand and turned her back to him. Feeling his fingers fumble with the clasp, Hannah couldn't help shivering as they brushed against her sensitive skin. When he got it secured, she turned to him, fingering the cross. "How does it look?"

"Beautiful," he said.

Everything, the look in his eyes, the sweet smile on his face, and the soft touch of his fingers on the back of her hand, told her he wasn't referring to the necklace. And for the moment, that was exactly how she felt.

They spent another hour on the hood of his Camaro, watching the planes fly overhead, talking and laughing into the summer night air. As much as she hated the evening to end, Hannah knew she had to get this awful thing over with. "Ready to go?" she asked.

"Yeah, I wouldn't want to bring you home so late that your dad flips out."

Hannah forced a smile. Her dad wasn't the one she was worried would flip out. They got into the car and headed down the quiet streets toward her house. The night had closed in on them. No more bright colorful lights of the carnival, no more hoots and hollers of delight, no more merry-go-round music. Linbeck was closed, and its residents had retreated to their homes.

When they reached her darkened house, Hannah was relieved to see that her father hadn't waited up, as she'd expected. Maybe that was proof he believed her when she'd promised to make things right between her and Josh tonight.

"I had a good time tonight." Hannah smiled at Josh through soft shadows between them.

He nodded. "So did I."

When she hesitated to leave, Josh said, "I heard your dad as we left, reminding you to tell me something." He waited a tick in time. "So...?"

Hannah felt her heart drop as she looked into his expectant face. It was obvious he had no idea the news she was about to deliver wouldn't be good. How could she crush his spirit this way, after he'd made such an effort showing her a good time? Tomorrow would be soon enough to break his heart.

"I have no idea what he was talking about."

Josh frowned slightly. "But... he said it was important."

Hannah sighed and shook her head. She got out of the car and said, "Soon as I remember what it is, you'll be the first to know."

"Couldn't have been too important, then," he said, grinning. Putting the car in reverse, he quickly added, "I'll give you a call." He winked. "Soon." With that, he was gone, and took her heart with him.

~ FIVE ~

Hannah tilted the rearview mirror toward her and cleared her throat. "Josh, I'm pregnant." Shaking her head, she dropped her hand in her lap. *No, no,* she thought, *that's all wrong.* Lifting her chin slightly, she tried again. "Um, Josh? I'm, ah, pregnant..."

Glancing out the window, she exhaled a sigh of frustration. There was no easy way to tell him about the baby, but she had to. And soon. Their relationship had been growing steadily, turning into something deeper and more meaningful with each passing day. When they were together, the air between them felt electric, and with their lingering gazes and flirtatious grins, came a quiet dread of the moment she'd have to break the news to him. Several times, she'd tried and failed. No time ever seemed to be the right time.

When Josh had invited her to his apartment for a late lunch, Hannah knew she couldn't let another day pass without telling him. No more excuses, no more delays. She had a promise to her father yet to be fulfilled, and a conviction inside her that could no longer be ignored.

Now as she drove through Josh's neighborhood, a middle-class residential area of small brick homes, Hannah double-checked the house number he'd scrawled on a slip of scrap paper, and pulled into the driveway, she couldn't help smiling a bit, undeterred by the leaden feeling in her stomach. It was the rancher they'd toilet papered freshman year of high school. Mr. Owen, their science teacher, had given a few of them detention for what he termed "excessive laughter" in the back of the classroom, and they'd responded by decorating his house. Their deed, Hannah recalled, hadn't gone unpunished. When their parents got wind of it, every one of them was grounded for a week. *Leave it to Josh to buy the place.*

As she put the car in park and gathered the pan of

brownies she'd baked, Josh threw open the front door with a grin, wielding a pair of tongs in his hand. "I see you found the place."

Hannah shielded her eyes from the sun. "If you'd told me it was Mr. Owen's house, I wouldn't have needed directions."

Josh chuckled. "Every time I get the mail and look at that tree," he said, using the tongs as a pointer, "I remember our night on the wild side." He motioned her inside. "C'mon, I'll give you a tour."

Then he spied the pan in her hands and relieved her of it. "What have we got here?" e peeked under the lid, then looked up at her with appreciation. "My favorite. Thanks."

Josh brought the brownies to the kitchen, and Hannah's gaze followed the wide chair rails toward high ceilings and arched windows. Josh had painted the walls a soft tan and furnished the living room with chocolate brown leather couches, a huge television, and Bohemian décor. She never would have guessed he'd have such good taste.

"Nice," she said, nodding. "Very tidy, too."

"What were you expecting?" He chuckled when he saw her face. "Your typical bachelor?"

Hannah only shrugged, afraid to admit that she'd stereotyped him. She followed him through the living room and down the hall to his office. Framed photos of him in exotic places adorned the desk shelves. Hannah inspected a picture of Josh, holding a dark-haired little girl on his lap. She was obviously malnourished and weak, yet her smile glowed with energy and enthusiasm, inspired by the handsome young man beside her. The joy gleaming in her dark eyes was so innocent and pure it took Hannah's breath away. How could this child seem so happy amidst poverty and sickness, while Hannah, who'd never experienced hunger or thirst, had struggled all her life to find that kind of peace and contentment?

"That's Aazzi," Josh said. "I met her on my first trip

to Guatemala. She followed me everywhere I went, curious to hear anything I had to say. If I could've, I would've taken her home with me." There was no mistaking the sadness and regret in his voice, and Hannah knew he meant every word.

"It's amazing, all the things you've done and the places you've gone."

With a nod, Josh invited her to follow him into the next room. "You haven't exactly been a homebody, yourself."

"It's not the same, and you know it," she said, one step behind him. "All your travels meant something. You've done something with your life." She sighed. "My trips were..." *Self-serving*, she admitted dismally. Shaking her head, she added, "My trips were pure fun. No one got anything out of them. Except me."

Shoving open the bedroom door, Josh looked at her. "You sell yourself short, Baby. You're amazing. And it isn't too late, you know, for you to make something of your life."

"You always know the right thing to say. It's a gift I wasn't given, I'm afraid."

She couldn't bear the intensity of his gaze another moment, so to avoid it, Hannah stepped into the room. No one who knew him could mistake it for a guest room. Everything about it was Josh. Sunlight spilled through a large window on one wall, basking the room with light. Oversized oak furniture made the room feel cozy rather than small, and the bed was neatly made with shades of tan. She felt the beginnings of a blush, and averted her gaze. Hopefully, he hadn't noticed that the sight of his queen-sized mattress had made her blush.

"Very nice," she mumbled, her eyes on the floor.

"Glad you approve," he said with a smile. And heading down the hall, he added, "Hungry?"

Hannah followed the delicious aromas wafting through the house. Thankfully, her wanton thoughts hadn't been that obvious.

The instant she set foot in the kitchen, Hannah felt a sense of place, felt like she'd come home. Warm yellow walls trimmed in bright white welcomed her like a comforting hug. Wide French doors opened to a deck and fenced backyard. On a small patio just beyond the deck sat the smoking grill. Closing her eyes, she inhaled the scents of sizzling chicken and seasoned vegetables. So, besides being a truly nice guy who knew how to keep himself neat and tidy, he could cook.

She was about to ask if there was anything he couldn't do when Josh motioned her to a cushioned patio chair and flicked on the small radio beside the doors. As the music softly played in the background, he lifted the grill's lid and waved away a thick cloud of white smoke. The sudden aroma wafting through the air stirred an unexpected memory, one that hurt to remember.

Driving to a study date with a friend one evening while in college, she had passed the local dive, Country Chicken. The stale and greasy aroma of the cooking poultry polluted the air and drew her attention to the gray Ford, parked haphazardly in the front row. Without a second glance, she'd known it was her then-boyfriend Ben's truck. Turning into the lot with the intention of surprising him, she spotted them. Stephanie and Ben, feasting on chicken that made their lips look wet with grease as they talked and laughed together. Their heads were bent close in a gesture that screamed more than just friends. That'd been the first time her heart broke.

"Hannah? Can I get you anything to drink?" Josh asked, eyeing her curiously as he turned a golden chicken breast.

"Oh, sorry," she said, snapping out of her reverie. "I'd love some ice water. But let me get it since you're doing everything else." She liked the expression her offer put on his handsome face. Not gratitude, more like...love. Could it be?

"I'll have one, too, if you don't mind," he said. "Just rummage around until you find what you need. Make yourself at home."

Hannah stepped into the kitchen, trying to guess which cupboard the glasses would be in. A box of *Captain Crunch* caught her eye, causing her to smile. Apparently, the boy in him hadn't died completely. She decided to try the most sensible option, and that was to check out the cupboard closest to the sink. While she found a shelf of glasses, she also found Josh's goody stash of *Oreos* and *Little Debbie* chocolate donuts, a weakness he'd carried with him from childhood. She liked this side of Josh that she was seeing. Behind his gorgeous face, pretty house, and wonderful life, there was a real man, complete with imperfections and quirks.

Opening his freezer to get some ice, Hannah found an assortment of healthy fruit and vegetables in addition to frozen steaks and beef. She was one who liked her frozen dinners and five-minute meals, like spaghetti. She took her *Woman's One a Day* vitamin and never spared more time than she had to on cooking or eating. Again, it reminded her of why she'd always liked Josh so much—he was her happy medium.

Hannah poured water into each glass, watching the ice crackle and snap. As she did so, a familiar song began playing in the background. *Abandoned Love*. Bob Dylan's voice reminded her of the inevitable conversation she would be having with Josh before the day's end. This same voice, she recalled, had sang to her from behind her closed dorm room door the night her heart had broken a second time. Over the haunting words she'd heard Ben and Stephanie's laughter and as the door slowly swung open, revealing Hannah's new truth - that she was pregnant and completely alone - Bob had sung out, *"Everybody's wearing a disguise, to hide what they've got left behind their eyes. But me, I can't cover what I am..."*

She set the glasses on the countertop, coming to the

realization that she had a long way to go to be worthy of a guy like Josh. It saddened her, but she had a lot of growing up to do and a baby on the way. Hannah wondered if she could do it quickly enough, thoroughly enough, to earn Josh's love. Deciding to start right then, she grabbed a couple of plates from the cupboard and gathered the utensils. Placing them neatly on the table, she arranged the already prepared salad, fresh fruit, and beans around until it looked perfect.

Hannah delivered his ice water while Josh balanced the last piece of chicken on the platter, and then surrounded it with steaming squash and zucchini. "Hope you have an appetite."

Ruminating about her past and the state of her character was anything but appetizing. But food would take her mind off the facts about her future, at least for as long as the meal lasted.

"Wow," he said, sliding the platter onto the table. "Look what you did." Josh faced her. "Who knew you had a domestic side!"

She knew he'd meant it as a joke. Still, his comment stung. How had she let her life, herself, get so out of control that setting a table came as a surprise to those who knew her?

"Have a seat and dish up," he said, reaching into the freezer for more ice.

As if on autopilot, Hannah sat on the nearest chair and began piling food on her plate. Soon, the pile of food threatened to overflow the edge of the dish. "Everything looks delicious," she said, hoping the nervousness she felt wasn't obvious in her voice.

Suddenly, he was behind her, so close that his warm breath sent shivers down her spine. "You look like you're eating for two," he joked.

This time, it wasn't so easy to ignore his attempt at humor. Hannah's stomach lurched as she dropped the serving spoon back into the salad bowl. She managed a nervous laugh and leaned away from him. "I... I haven't eaten all day."

He sat across from her and loaded up his own plate. "No offense. Guess I forgot what a healthy appetite you have." She managed a feeble smile. "So, heard from any of the employers you interviewed with?" he asked.

Hannah slid a cherry tomato around her plate, suddenly wishing she hadn't said yes to this invitation. "I'm keeping my eye on the paper and the Internet, but haven't found anything yet."

He bit off a mouthful of chicken. "You looking around Linbeck or... not?"

She jabbed her fork into the tomato. "I'm sticking around."

Josh stopped chewing and gave her a long, thoughtful look. "You don't sound too thrilled about it."

What was there to be thrilled about? She'd come back to the place where her mother had deserted her, jobless, pregnant, unmarried, and falling in love with a guy who didn't deserve to be saddled with the likes of her. "I hear it's going to rain tonight," she said, forcing cheerfulness she didn't feel into her voice.

Josh observed her for a few endless seconds, questions flashing across his face. Instead of pursuing the issue, though, he held his hands up in mock surrender. "I can take a hint."

Hannah was grateful for his conversational skills, for him expertly steering the discussion from politics to weather and goings-on at the church. His stories mesmerized her, delighted her, had her laughing so hard she had to use her napkin to daub tears from her eyes. This is how life with_ Josh would be, she told herself. Why wish for the impossible? Life with Josh was out of the question.

Half an hour later, Josh stood to clear the table. "Sure you had enough to eat?"

Hannah nodded. "More than enough. It was fantastic."

He started filling the dishwasher, but she playfully batted his hands from the plates. "Let me clean up," she said. And when he hesitated, she added, "It's the least I can do. Just sit there and keep me company until the job's done."

Just as she hoped, Josh entertained her with more stories, and the time passed quickly. Too quickly. It's now or never, she thought.

Walking reluctantly to the table, Hannah sat in the chair beside his. "Josh, there's something I have to talk to you about."

"It sounds important." His brow raised curiously.

Hannah bit her lower lip. "Very serious," she said, wringing her hands together.

Josh leaned back in his chair and crossed both arms over his chest. "I'm all ears."

She took a deep breath, trying to remember which of her rehearsals had turned out best. "I guess there's no way to say this, except to blurt it out." She met his unwavering gaze and said, "I'm... pregnant."

The only sound in the room was the steady tick-tock of the clock above the stove. And her hammering heartbeat. Why wasn't he saying something? Why was he staring at her that way, with a blank expression that told her nothing?

"You're kidding, right?"

Hannah shook her head, already feeling devastated at his reaction. She'd expected it, but had hoped for something else.

Josh exhaled sharply and stared at some invisible spot between his shoes, his powerful jaw clenching and unclenching. "How long have you known?" he asked flatly.

She hesitated. "About two months."

Josh leaned closer, finally meeting her gaze with hard eyes. "Why didn't you tell me right away?"

"What did you expect me to do? Waltz into town, after we hadn't talked in years, and say 'Oh hey, nice seeing you again. And by the way... I'm pregnant?'"

Shaking his head slowly, he muttered something un-intelligible. "I have to admit, I would have preferred that announcement to this one."

She tried to read his face, but he hid it behind his hand. "It isn't something I'm proud of," Hannah admitted, hearing her voice waver.

Finally, he looked at her again. "So," he began, "all this time, every time we were together, all the flirting and...." He ran a hand through his hair. "...And you never thought to tell me you're pregnant?"

Hannah's shoulders drooped. "You have to believe me, Josh. I tried to tell you, dozens of times. I just couldn't seem to find the right words, or the right time. I never expected to feel... I didn't think you and I would..." She took a deep breath and blinked back the tears that stung her eyes. "This just—"

"Happened," he finished, cutting her off. "It always does."

"Please don't be mad at me, Josh. You're a pastor. You of all people should understand that people make mis-takes," Hannah said desperately.

He got up slowly and headed for the front door, and she knew he intended to ask her to leave. "Leading me on wasn't a mistake," he said over his shoulder.

She ran around in front of him and placed a hand on his chest. "I wasn't leading you on," she said quietly.

"Then what, exactly, were you doing?"

She shrugged miserably. The truth was, she'd been lonely. Afraid. Angry. And being with Josh felt so good. Made her feel good about herself... something she hadn't felt in a long, long time. It had been selfish to use him that way, she realized, too late. "I guess," she said haltingly, "I was hoping to make up for lost time."

His eyes searched her face, then he looked toward the ceiling, as if hoping to find answers to his questions written up there. "Maybe your time would have been better spent if you'd spent it with the baby's father instead of me."

Traitorous tears welled in her eyes and, though she tried to stop them, they spilled onto her cheeks. Hannah didn't even bother to wipe them away. Instead, she grabbed her purse and hurried out the door. In the car, she fumbled with her keys as sobs shook her body. Finally, thankfully, she found the ignition and backed out of the driveway. It was happening again.

The day she'd told Ben of her suspicions about the pregnancy, he'd withdrawn from her, too. He'd turned cold and stony, though she hadn't even taken the test yet. She could be wrong, she tried to explain, but Ben insisted he'd been down that road before. He knew what a week late meant, and he wouldn't let her mistake mess up the rest of his life.

The whole scene had been so surreal that Hannah couldn't believe it had actually happened. Surely it had just been a dream. A terrible nightmare. So she'd left his dorm room and headed straight to the drug store, determined to bring him proof that it had all been a terrible mistake.

But once she got there, she couldn't bring herself to go in. The thought of buying a test, alone, was so daunting that she'd sat in her car for what seemed like hours, staring inside the store's front window as the blinking neon from the 'open' sign mesmerized her. Finally, what was actually twenty minutes later, Hannah had slowly pulled out and driven home, her future seeming as empty as she felt inside.

Now, as Hannah pulled into her drive, she remained rooted to the seat of her dad's Oldsmobile. It may as well have been that night all over again, when Ben threw her out of his life without a passing thought. And now Josh. She glanced at herself in the rearview mirror, and even in the fading light, saw her blotchy face and smeared mascara. She'd already upset Josh. The last thing Hannah wanted was to begin a repeat performance with her dad. She'd go to the river, the only place where she'd ever felt at peace.

By now, the sun had reached the horizon, so low it created a hazy glow that settled above the ground. Fingers of sunlight still clung to the sky, making it look as fresh and radiant as a painting.

The river wound its way through the trees, catching the sun in its cradle as it disappeared in the falling darkness. Ripples silently waved their course downstream, and there was the sound of a drip or swirl of the water. The tree frogs began their night song as the hum of crickets harmonized in the background.

Hannah watched the sun wink its final goodbye and as the eddy of colors faded away, a deep, satiny expanse of space was left. Thousands of stars dotted the dark canopy, as far as the eye could see, and Orion, a magnificent giant, stood out like the king of the sky. When the darkness was complete, fireflies began to drift through the shadows like hundreds of tiny lanterns floating on the breeze.

This secret place she and Josh had grown up loving used to make her feel so alive. Now, it just made her feel alone.

Over the four years she'd been away, she'd lost touch with every friend she'd grown up with. Then throughout college her friends graduated or transferred, or in Stephanie's case, slept with her boyfriend. In the end, Hannah walked away with no one except her dad and Josh. She realized that by not telling Josh sooner, she may have possibly put an end to the one relationship that meant the most to her, aside from her father's. A part of her had hoped that Josh would love her (baby or no baby), just as she was. A part of her told her that if it weren't for the baby, he would have.

The sound of soft footfalls interrupted her thoughts. She turned, startled to see Josh walking toward her. He stopped a few feet behind her, looking uncomfortable, and saying nothing for a few awkward seconds. Hannah turned her back to him and stared at the river winding its way through the shadows. After a minute, Josh sat beside her, elbows on his knees and staring at the darkness with her. Hastily she brushed at her tears. "I'm sorry," he said softly, looking straight ahead. "I didn't mean what I said and I didn't mean to make you cry."

Hannah didn't trust herself to speak, so she didn't. She felt his eyes on her as the tears welled up again.

"Hannah," he said, draping an arm across her shoulders. "Come here." Pulling her to him, he held her tenderly as she cried in fear, uncertainty, and loneliness for herself and her unborn baby. Finally, she pulled away, embarrassed by her show of weakness.

"Do you want to talk about it?"

She hesitated, but only for a second. The burden of her situation weighed on her and she felt the need to share with someone. More so, she felt she owed Josh an explanation. "I haven't heard from Ben since I told him I might be pregnant. I've tried calling a dozen times, but he doesn't answer. I don't expect him to do anything for me, but the baby deserves to live a good life, and he owes it that." She sighed. "I'm such an idiot," she said, trying to hide the waver in her voice. "I trusted him. With far too much."

"If you don't mind me asking," Josh said cautiously, "How long were you two together?"

Hannah hesitated. A part of her didn't want to dredge up memories of Ben. "Off and on for three years. I found out he'd been sleeping with my roommate for the better part of it. Seemed they were both pretty good at keeping secrets," Hannah admitted, the hurt so fresh it stung.

Josh sat silent for a moment, as if contemplating his next question. Finally, he asked, "Do you love him?"

She thought for a moment, wanting to choose her words carefully. It was important to her that Josh knew she no longer had romantic feelings toward Ben. That what had

77

seemingly developed between her and Josh had been real and not a rebound for her. "No," she answered. "And honestly, in hindsight, I never did."

Josh tossed a few pebbles into the water. "Have you thought about what you're going to do?"

"I've considered adoption but I'm so afraid that I'll regret it. I mean, for the rest of my life, I'll know I have a child out there who's part of me. Then, what if I keep it? What if I'm like my mother, and I can't give it the love-"

Josh elbowed her gently, interrupting her. "Hey, slow down. Nothing to do now but take it one day at a time. Time and prayer, that's all you need. In a couple months, you'll have everything figured out."

Hannah turned slightly to face him. "You think so?" Josh nodded. "I sure hope you're right." She picked at the grass. "Don't be mad at me," she said quietly. "I hate that I've disappointed and hurt you, and I'm so sorry..."

Josh scooted closer to her and put his arm around her waist. "I'm not mad at you. I couldn't stay mad at you four years ago when you left me, and I can't be mad at you now." He chuckled quietly. "I am a pastor after all."

Hannah ducked her head. "That was a stupid thing to say. Sorry." She managed a smile.

"So," Josh said. "Have you seen the doctor yet?"

Shaking her head, she plucked a week from the ground and rolled it between her fingers. "Monday is my first appointment."

He paused. "Is Michael going with you?"

"No. He's working." She tossed the weed aside.

"Promise me something." Hannah turned to Josh, catching his eye.

After a slight hesitation, he nodded.

"Promise me we'll always be friends," she said sincerely.

Looking slightly relieved, Josh grinned and slid his arm around her shoulders again. "Promise."

Hannah leaned into him, thinking if it weren't for

the baby, they could be so much more.

~ SIX ~

Hannah woke up queasy, and none of the tricks she'd read online did anything to settle her stomach. As she hovered over the toilet, hoping the saltines and ginger ale wouldn't come up, she couldn't help but think how lucky she was—even with everything that was wrong with her life—to have a friend like Josh. While her hopes at something more had all but dissipated after their confrontation, Hannah felt relieved that he was at least giving their friendship a second chance.

Of course, she'd noticed the change in him. There were no more flirtatious gestures, accidental touches, or meaningful gazes. He'd become a Josh she'd never experienced before, and she realized now that was because he'd loved her for so long that the only way he knew how to be with her was as a man in love. Now, he made it clear that they were just friends. And while it hurt her deep inside that this was one of the many consequences she'd brought on herself by her irresponsible actions, she held on to the gratitude that Josh was still willing to be in her life.

The instant he'd heard she couldn't use her dad's car to get to her doctor's appointment on Monday morning, he'd offered to drive her, refusing to take no for an answer. Although she'd thanked him and insisted she couldn't let him neglect his work for that long, he still wouldn't cave. "Consider it my apology," he'd said, "for behaving like such a jerk when you told me about the baby."

And right on schedule, he showed up early Monday morning. "I brought breakfast," he called through the screen.

"Come in," she hollered back. "I'm...ah...I'll be out in a minute."

"Hey," he said, suddenly standing in the bathroom door. "Not feeling so well, huh?"

Hannah slumped to the floor. "Penance, I guess," she said with a slight smile.

He shook a brown paper bag and held out the cardboard tray balanced on his right palm. "I brought breakfast... bagels and hot tea."

Would she ever get over how sweet he could be? *Nothing like Ben,* she thought. Selfishness like Ben's was one of a kind. Like the occasion her tire blew on Interstate 55 and she'd called him for help. Unfortunately for her, the Bears were playing the Packers and he'd told her he'd be there in a few minutes, but forty-five minutes later he still hadn't showed and wouldn't answer his phone. So, she'd spent the entire afternoon on the side of the highway until a friend was able to pick her up.

"Thanks," Hannah mumbled, standing to uncap the tea. A glance at her watch told her they had ten minutes before they'd needed to leave.

"Guess you don't feel much like eating a bagel, huh?"

"Maybe later. Now if you'll excuse me for a minute," she said, gently pushing him toward the door, "I have to finish getting ready." He passed her an understanding smile as the door clicked shut.

She pulled her hair into a ponytail and applied some mascara, hoping it would draw attention from her pale complexion. Seeing that nothing would do the trick, she brushed her teeth instead. Untucking her shirt from her jeans' waistband and groaning, she shook her head. It was happening already. All her clothes were getting snug. And how in the world was she going to afford maternity clothes when she didn't have a job? The silly adage from *The Lion King* resonated in her brain: Hakuna Matata. *No worries,* she thought, heading for the living room. At least not right now.

She found that Josh had made himself comfortable. Feet propped on the ottoman, he sat munching a bagel, absent-mindedly flipping through TV channels.

"Ready?" she asked, grabbing her purse.

Josh yawned and stretched when he stood. "You

81

look a little less green."

"It comes and goes." She opened the door to dreary, gray skies and waited for Josh to step onto the porch before locking it behind them.

"Let's hope it's gone during the drive." His eyes were wide as if to stress the importance.

"I'll do my best."

"To puke in my car?"

"No," Hannah said, laughing, "not to."

As they drove, Josh hummed and drummed his fingers on the steering wheel in time with *Tainted Love*, filtering softly from the radio.

Hannah watched the cloudy skies outside. They reminded her of the morning she sat in the Dean's office, the day after she'd discovered Ben and Stephanie together in her room.

"Hannah," Mr. Craft had said, looking at her with kind eyes. "Graduation is two days away. In any other circumstance, I would have to take further disciplinary actions, but seeing how you're an honor grad, I won't."

Keeping her eyes averted to her lap where her bruised knuckles rested, Hannah asked quietly, "So I'll graduate?"

"Yes, you will. Meanwhile, stay away from Ben and Stephanie. They've agreed to do the same. Stephanie has already moved her stuff from the room." He paused before adding, "Let this be a warning. If you go near either of them, they've threatened to press charges."

As if I ever want to see them again, she'd thought, fighting back tears.

She remembered wishing that instead of rain, the clouds would open and swallow her, taking her away from the pain she felt, the betrayal, and pour her out somewhere peaceful, maybe in another state or continent. Somewhere the skies weren't forlorn and her heart somber.

"Baby," Josh said softly. "We're here."

Dread settled over her as she stared at the brown

brick building towering in front of her. Framed by the billowing gray clouds, it was the perfect picture of her mood. A sign directed her to Dr. Miller's office on the first floor.

"Ready or not," she droned, unbuckling her seatbelt. And as she got out of the car, it dawned on her that if Josh came inside, everyone would think he was the baby's father. Considering he was a youth pastor in a small town like Linbeck, she didn't think it would be the best idea. "I won't be long," she said. "Maybe you can drive to a 7-11 or something, buy yourself something to read while you—"

"Are you kidding? You look like you might pass out any minute. I'm going in."

"But Josh," she began, looking over her shoulder at the packed parking lot, "what will people think?"

"If I cared about stuff like that, I wouldn't have offered to bring you here." He locked the car and ushered her up the narrow sidewalk.

All Hannah could do was sigh and go along with him. It's what she'd been doing all her life, after all. Being a follower had put her into some sticky situations, but she'd never been the type who could just say no.

In the brightly lit office, Dr. Miller's receptionist handed her a clipboard and explained how to fill out the forms while Josh took a seat in the nearest chair and picked up a copy of *Parenting*. Hannah sat beside him and scribbled furiously, feeling fidgety and anxious. "Not much of a selection of manly reading material," she said, apologetically. She felt like she should be excusing the office for their lack of hospitality to men, namely Josh. He had, after all, gone out of his way to help her.

He met her eyes. "So will you see it today? The baby, I mean?"

Hannah felt herself warm inside at his question. She was touched that he cared enough to ask. And honestly, she hadn't thought about what might happen during today's appointment. "I don't think so. I think today is just a routine checkup."

Josh nodded and turned his attention to the magazine as Hannah finished her paperwork. A second later, the
front door jingled open and a very pregnant girl waddled
in, followed by an awkward looking man. She watched as
the girl signed the time in form and exchanged warm greet-
ings with the receptionist. The instant they sat, their fingers wove together and they leaned close to one another,
whispering like best friends. Hannah couldn't help but
wonder how the pretty girl with her round, brown eyes and
curly hair ended up with the wiry young man who looked
like he couldn't even grow facial hair yet. Wait, Hannah
squinted a little. She did see a smidgen of fine hairs on his
upper lip. Silently, she scolded herself. Perhaps her obser-
vation was merely the byproduct of jealousy. Hannah
yearned for love like that, so much that she felt the heat of
her envy knotting in her stomach.

"Did you know that constant thirst is a sign of diabetes?" Josh said, pointing at the article on juvenile diabetes.

Startled by his unintended interruption, Hannah
blinked her eyes and sat up straighter. "What? Oh, no, I
didn't know that."

Just then a door in the corner of the office opened
and a nurse called her name. "This shouldn't take long,"
she told Josh, getting to her feet.

"I have no place to go," he mumbled, his attention
on the article again.

Hannah passed through the door, held by the nurse.

"And how are you today, darlin'?" Her name tag
said Suanne. A nice name. Different. She tried it out—
Suanne Sinclair—and decided she'd keep searching.

"I've been better," Hannah said, dropping her purse
on a nearby stool. "Morning sickness is no friend of mine."

Suanne led her to the scale. "Don't worry, it gets
better. Time to take off your shoes and step up, honey."

So it got better, did it? Only to be replaced by back-
aches and swollen ankles and cravings for chocolate covered pickles. One foot after the other, she got onto the

scale. "That's good news."

Suanne scribbled on the chart, then pointed at a wheeled stool. "Now if you'll have a seat, I'll get your blood pressure."

Pulse, weight, blood pressure. Once all Hannah's numbers were recorded, the nurse showed her to the exam room. "Everything off, dear, and put on this lovely paper gown. The doc will be with you shortly." As Suanne turned to leave, she added, "Congratulations on your pregnancy."

Congratulations, indeed, Hannah thought, once again following instructions. She did her best to keep the gown in place without tearing it. Looking around, she noticed tongue depressors, surgical gloves, and on the ceiling, a sprinkler. What happens if there's a fire right now, she wondered. The image of her scurrying in the paper gown toward the exit made her cringe inwardly.

She listened attentively to muffled voices in the exam room beside hers, footsteps in the hallway, the distant ringing of the phone. She wished Josh was beside her, taking her mind off the taupe walls decorated with Anne Geddes posters and diagrams of the female body. As she was reaching for a tattered magazine, a quick tap on the door startled her so badly she nearly toppled off the exam table.

Dr. Miller entered, Hannah's chart balanced on one forearm as he flipped through the pages. "Doctor Miller," he said, extending his hand. "Sorry for the delay. How is everything going? Any problems, questions, concerns?"

Questions? She had a million. Problems? She had two million of those. As for concerns, Hannah didn't think the numbering system went that high. But she shook her head instead. "Except for morning sickness, everything has been fine."

"Good, good," he said, glancing at her records again. "You're eight weeks along as of Wednesday, so today's appointment will be pretty short and sweet. We'll do a routine exam, then set up an appointment for next month. Sound good?"

Hannah nodded curtly, keeping her eyes on the ceiling as the doctor snapped on a pair of Latex gloves and began the exam. Hannah saw his frown immediately. "Something wrong?"

He pulled the gloves off and tossed them in the trash. "How long have you been spotting?"

"Spotting? I didn't notice any—"

He washed his hands. "It isn't much, and probably isn't serious. But I'm going to do an ultrasound to check things out in there, though."

Hannah watched as he wheeled the machine over and plugged it in. The screen came to life as he adjusted the bar. There was the brief moment when nothing made sense, and then they were staring at a tiny dot, tucked deep in her womb. The doctor moved the bar around at various angles until he was satisfied.

"Everything looks fine," he said, looking at the screen. He continued studying the pictures, then turned everything off and wheeled the machine back to its corner.

"Just keep a close eye on things," he instructed, waving a finger under her nose. "If you notice the spotting getting worse, you start cramping or anything, give us a call."

"What does it mean?" she asked. "The spotting, that is."

"Ninety-nine percent of the time, it's nothing." He patted her hand reassuringly. "Long as you take it easy— that means no mountain climbing and skydiving—things should settle down. As long as we keep a close eye on it, you and your baby should be fine."

You and your baby. Despite his assurances, Hannah was worried, because a sudden surge of protectiveness rose up inside her. Was it proof she hadn't inherited her mother's lack of maternal skills? Could she love this child, nurture and care for it, until it was all grown up and on its own?

"Thanks, Dr. Miller."

"After you're dressed, stop by the desk on your way out and have Jan schedule your next appointment. I want to see you in two weeks, to check on things. If everything is okay after that, we'll start seeing you monthly." He winked. "Until the delivery day gets closer, that is." He scribbled something on a prescription pad. "I want you to have this filled, and take two a day, every day. Vitamins are essential, especially in the first trimester." And with that, he turned to leave, his white coat flapping behind him.

She dressed slowly, not wanting to do anything that might cause the bleeding to worsen. When she entered the waiting room, Josh dropped his magazine on an end table and stood.

"Well?" He grinned.

"Everything's fine. Just fine." She didn't trust herself to explain things here, in the doctor's office. The last thing she needed right now was an audience listening to her physical problems.

After setting up her next appointment, she and Josh walked wordlessly back to his car. Hannah could feel Josh's eyes on her, but he remained silent as he unlocked the doors and they climbed in.

Fastened securely in his seat, Josh waited until she settled in to ask, "You sure everything is fine?"

Hannah glanced at him, knowing he detected her unease. "More or less," she replied. For some reason she was having a difficult time forming words for how she felt.

"More or less," Josh echoed. And though he tried to say it quietly, so she wouldn't hear him, Hannah heard him whisper "More secrets. Great. Just great."

Josh remained quiet the entire ride home. Hannah, meanwhile, couldn't decide what the best thing to do was. Worry Josh with the truth, which could be nothing? Or keep the precautionary stuff Dr. Miller had told her to herself, until they knew more about what was going on inside her?

Leaning against the headrest, she closed her eyes,

picturing the little dot on the monitor that was her baby. Soon, it would develop arms and legs, fingers and toes. It would squirm and kick, and then—

And then she'd have to figure out how to feed and clothe the baby. Find someone trustworthy to take care of it while she worked to pay the bills. It was scary. And a little exciting. Wonderful. And horrible. She didn't know if she could do it.

She glanced at Josh's handsome profile. With friends like him, and a loving dad, she might be able to pull it off. It wouldn't be easy, of course, but her father had managed to raise her single-handedly, after her so-called mother ran off and left them. Maybe, just maybe, Hannah had inherited her dad's parenting skills, not her mother's.

Suddenly, exhaustion overwhelmed her. All she wanted right now was to curl up under the covers and sleep. Maybe, if she were lucky, the answers to all her questions, the solutions to all her problems would come to her in a dream. And maybe the spotting was a one-time thing. Her baby would grow and thrive, and—

"I know you said everything is fine," Josh said as he pulled into her drive. "But something didn't go right in there. You want to talk about it?"

She forced a cheerful smile, not wanting to burden him with her inner war. "I'm fine. It's a lot to absorb in such a short time. And I was up half the night feeling sick, so I'm worn out."

Instantly, his handsome features relaxed. It made her feel good that her little fib had relieved him of his worry over her. She got out of the car. "Thanks, Josh, for taking me. Tomorrow, how about if I fix you lunch, to show my appreciation?"

"Remember the time you tried to make lasagna for me?"

Hannah laughed. "The fire chief told me to stay out of the kitchen. Guess I'd better check with him before I cook."

He laughed, too. "Call me if you need anything."

Hannah blew him a kiss. "You know I will."

Waving as he backed out of the drive, Hannah felt an overwhelming need to lie down. Inside, without bothering to lock the door or change clothes, she collapsed onto her bed and almost instantly fell asleep.

~ * ~

When Hannah opened her eyes, she saw nothing but a thin streak of light sneaking in through the slight opening in her bedroom door. She rolled over, feeling nauseous and disoriented. The numerals of her alarm glowed bright red, burning 9:45 into the surrounding darkness.

A slow ache swirled through her abdomen as she sat up and tossed the covers aside. Even that slight movement caused the pain to double in intensity. Taking slow, small steps, she made her way to the bathroom, covering her eyes when she flipped on the light. That's when she noticed the blood staining her pants and felt it running down her leg.

Hannah opened the bathroom door and saw the trail of blood from her bedroom. Dizzy, she leaned against the wall, fighting the darkness that threatened to overtake her.

"Dad!" Hannah managed, but her voice sounded weak and distant. "Dad!"

There's so much blood. Using the wall for support, Hannah made it down the hallway and down a few steps, leaving a blood trail behind her. Halfway downstairs, she saw her dad reading in his chair.

"Dad, something's wrong," Hannah cried.

He looked alarmed as he jumped to his feet. "What is it? What's wrong?" he asked, rushing toward her as she felt the darkness suddenly close in on her.

A sharp flash of light blinded her for a split second before she regained consciousness at the bottom of the stairs. Once again, clouds of hazy blackness threatened to overcome her, but she fought it long enough to feel the ex-

plosive pain in her stomach. She could hear her dad's pan-
icked voice, dimming, then growing louder, as she went in
and out of consciousness.

The next thing she knew, someone slid an oxygen
mask over her face. Her dad was hovering over her, his
face set in fear. That was the last thing she remembered
until she came to in the hospital.

Hannah had no idea how long she'd been there. She
struggled to open her eyes and push the fatigue away.
Moaning slightly at the sharp pain that shot through her
head, she touched the tender spot on her forehead and felt
a bandage covering a tender lump. Glancing around the
dimly lit room, she noticed a sliver of gray sky, peeking
through a crack in the window blinds.

Her dad snored softly in the small chair beside her
bed, a tiny blanket tucked under his chin. *Even in slumber,
he looks so sad,* she thought. His salt-and-pepper hair was
mussed, his clothes rumpled, his glasses askew. It seemed
he sensed her studying him, and his eyes fluttered open,
looking directly at her. He scooted the chair closer, and
wiped the sleep from his eyes. "Hey, hon. How are you
feeling?" he asked, his gray eyes searching her face.

"I'm okay, I guess. But what happened?"

Shifting uncomfortably in the chair, he said, "You
fainted and fell down the steps. Put quite a knot on your
head, young lady. It took eight stitches to sew you up."

Instinct forced her fingers to the bandage as she
took a deep breath. "And the baby?"

Averting his gaze, he shook his head. When he
looked at her, tears misted his eyes. "They think you were
miscarrying when you woke up earlier," he said, blanketing
her hand with his own "The loss of blood caused you to
pass out. When you fell…" His voice trailed off, and he
hung his head.

"It's gone?" she whispered. "I lost the baby?"

Nodding, he said, "I'm afraid so."

Hannah stared hard at their hands, entwined on the

blanket. If this had happened two weeks ago, she might have felt a twinge of relief. But when she'd seen the baby during the ultrasound, a strange new feeling had begun to take root in her heart.

"Josh is here," her father said.

Relief surged over her like an ocean wave. "I'd like to see him."

Her dad reached out, tenderly tucking a tendril of hair behind her ear, then stood and said, "I'll go get him."

Moments later, the door swooshed open again, and in walked Josh, head down and fingertips tucked into his jeans pockets. He must have been out there, waiting all night, because he looked as exhausted as she felt.

"Your dad went to get some coffee," he said, sitting in the chair beside the bed. Leaning forward, he took her hands between his own. "You doing okay?"

Blinking, she bit her lower lip, hoping to staunch the tears that stung behind her eyelids. "Did... did Dad tell you what happened?"

Josh nodded. "He called me from the hospital last night. I came right over, in case..." He gave her hands a gentle squeeze. "In case you needed me." Then he leaned down, resting his forehead against hers. "I'm sorry, Hannah."

"Thanks," she said, his action so tender it replaced a little of her ache. "I was so confused and afraid yesterday, not knowing how I'd get a job, how I'd take care of the baby, all by myself. And now..." She shrugged. "And now, I don't know what to feel."

He gave her hands another squeeze. "Like I said before, take it a day at a time. God will help you figure it out."

Later, as Hannah lay in the hospital bed alone, she thought about the baby she would never know and the life she'd begun to imagine with it. As she realized her life was back to what it was before that positive pregnancy test,

Hannah didn't feel relief at all. She'd changed her mind and her life around the baby, being forced to reassess who, and what she was. Now, Hannah was different from the girl she was two months ago. The least she could do for her father, and Josh, was to not go back to being the self-centered person she had been.

It was time to take control of her life again. This time around, she'd get a job, save money, and be prepared for her future. She'd help her father at the church, and Josh with his youth group, go to the homeless shelter without a complaint. She'd work on making other people's lives better, just as the two men in her life had done for her. And she knew she could do it, because as Josh had said, God would help her figure it all out.

~ SEVEN ~

"Time to go, Hannah. You've been here all day," Josh said irritably, trying to grab the remote out of her hand. "Or should I say, all week."

"And maybe I want to stay here the rest of the month." She leaned away from him, holding it just out of reach. "Who invited you over anyway?" she teased.

He snatched the remote from her. "I'm never invited over, you know that. Now c'mon. Let's go."

Hannah eyed him curiously. "Go where?" Then she smiled, sarcasm dripping from her voice. "Can't you see I'm busy?"

Under Josh's sudden intense scrutiny, she felt embarrassed as self-consciousness took over. Adjusting the collar of her robe and running a hand through her hair that was in desperate need of a shampoo, she followed his gaze around the room. Seeing the piles of *Kleenex*, she gathered the tissues from the couch and regretted her attempt of a joke.

"Yeah, you look it."

Hannah ignored him and turned back to her Lifetime show. "This is just getting good. Shannon found out that Luke is the one who took her baby."

Suddenly the TV went black. Hannah sat up quickly, spilling some tissues on the floor. Josh was still pointing the remote at the TV when she said, "Hey!"

"Let's go. I didn't come over here to watch you watch TV."

Again, Hannah glanced at Josh, curiosity welling up inside her. For the first time since he arrived, she noticed how good he looked. Dressed in a pair of khaki cargo pants and a white polo shirt with his hair looking styled and neat, Hannah knew he'd planned something special. And although she wasn't in much of a mood to go out, she would attempt it for Josh, whose assertiveness warmed her.

She recalled how earlier in the week Josh had shown

93

up sporting her favorite magazine, and a package of *Oreos* to feed her chocolate craving. Several times he'd even brought lunch or breakfast, but what Hannah had wanted, and appreciated the most, was his company.

Taking a seat on the ottoman, Josh scooted it so he was directly in front of her. His voice was patient and gentle as he said, "For your own good, I think it's time you get out of this house. It's been a week. You need some fresh air."

Hannah saw the sincerity and caring in his eyes, and loved him all the more for his forgiveness and friendship. She smiled slowly. "So where are we going?"

Grinning, Josh stood, pulling her up, too. "It's a surprise. So hurry up and get dressed."

"I should've known. With you, it's always a surprise," she said, still clutching at the collar of her robe. "You have any errands you need to run while I shower and change? It might take me a few—"

He waved a dismissive hand at her as he settled into the couch and flipped the TV back on. "Nah. I'll wait. I have to find out what happens to Luke and the baby, after all," he said with a wink.

Hannah giggled and headed up the stairs, suddenly excited for this mystery date. She hopped into the shower, and thought about Josh, her heart nearly bursting with happiness. All those years she'd spent without him, she felt as though something was missing in her life. Now she knew just how much she'd nearly lost.

Twenty minutes later, feeling fresh and clean, she spritzed on some perfume and went downstairs, hoping to redeem herself a little.

Josh stood when she hit the bottom step. "Wow," he said, smiling, "you clean up real good."

Hannah felt her heartbeat quicken. It was the closest thing to a flirtatious remark he'd offered since their confrontation. She'd chosen everything, from the color of her eye shadow to the shoes on her feet, because she knew

Josh liked them.

"Thanks. You get all dressed up for me?" she asked.

Grinning, Josh glanced around the room. "Must have, 'cause I don't see anyone else here."

She wondered if he considered this a date, or simply as two friends going out to have a good time. The thought of going on a date with Josh made butterflies take flight in her stomach. Maybe there was still hope.

Hannah held out her hand to him. Looking pleased, Josh took it. "Thanks for getting me off the couch. You were right – I need to get out."

Uncertainty and adoration flashed through his eyes simultaneously. At once, Hannah understood that while Josh was witnessing the changes in her personality, he was still leery of the relationship developing between them. It was a harsh reminder of the many mistakes she'd made until now. For so long, Hannah had been focused on doing whatever it took to not become her mother. And the past few years, she'd behaved in ways that almost made that inevitable. Silently, Hannah thanked God, while she and Josh walked hand-in-hand toward his car that He intervened in time. Pity that it took getting pregnant and losing the baby to wake her up, and if she hadn't been so hard-headed, it may not have taken a lesson so harsh. But it was what it was, and she was starting to find peace within herself.

Hannah was surprised to see the sun so low in the sky already. Climbing into his car, she spotted the picnic basket in the backseat. She turned to him, smiling. She felt a heart-swelling thrill. "You're taking me on a picnic?" She tried to hide the excitement in her voice, but failed.

Josh chuckled as stuffed the key into the ignition. "Hmm... what gave it away?"

"Oh," she gushed, "how cute."

"Not exactly the word I'd have chosen, but...." He stuck his hand behind his seat, felt around for a second, then withdrew a small bouquet of white irises. "If you'd call a picnic cute, what would you call this?"

Hannah felt the breath catch in her throat. He'd remembered that they were her favorite flowers. Her cheeks heated as she took them. Then she bit her lower lip to hide some of the unabashed joy she knew was written all over her face. "I'd call it sweet."

"Cute? Sweet?" He grinned and shook his head. "I was going for something more."

Hannah found herself wanting to tell him how grateful she was for him, how completely happy he made her, and how her life had felt so empty without him in it. Unable to trust herself to speak without putting her heart on her sleeve, Hannah leaned over and gave him a gentle peck on the cheek, instead.

Caught off guard, Josh's eyes lit up. They turned soft, almost tender. Something in them told her he was wishing for more. "That's more like it," he said. Josh fired up the car and, without another word, backed down the drive while Hannah sat back and pretended to watch her neighborhood whiz by through the passenger window. She thought about how close she'd come to kissing his lips, regretting that she didn't but grateful at the same time. Because, knowing Josh, he probably sensed that after all she'd been through recently with Ben and the baby, she wasn't ready for love and romance. What he didn't realize was that it was because of all she'd survived that Hannah understood how good Josh would be for her. But would she be good for him?

"Why so quiet?" he said, fiddling with the radio dials.

"Oh," she said, inhaling the sweet scent of the flowers, "just thinking."

He turned slightly and met her gaze for a moment. "About...?"

It surprised her, the way she felt all young and silly and shy, suddenly. Shrugging, she said, "Oh, I don't know. I've never been on a picnic at night before."

"Then you're in for a real treat. There's nothing nicer than eating under the moon and stars."

She couldn't help but wonder how he knew this. Had he brought other girls on moonlit picnics? Had he cared about them? A trace of jealousy coursed through her... an emotion she knew she had no right to feel, since she was the one who abandoned him. Right then, Hannah admitted to herself that she didn't deserve Josh. Instead, she would have to do what she could to earn his love. By the time Josh parked in town, Hannah was filled with resolve and determination, and she liked the feeling.

The sky was darkening. They walked and the street lamps clicked on, casting them in a dim, yellowish glow. Josh brought her to the only park in Linbeck, on one side of Main Street. She hadn't spent much time in the park in the past, other than an occasional walk-through with a friend, or to cut across to get to the *Dairy Queen* at the other end. It was fairly large with green grass and a few overgrown oaks. Benches were scattered throughout, placed strategically under the trees, and a small fountain that lit up at night occupied the center of the park.

Josh shook out a blanket and lay it in the grass, while Hannah rummaged through the basket. "Let's see what we've got. Ooh, I see you're aiming for a wild night." She pulled out a bottle of *Vandalia Cabernet*, a carbonated fruit juice.

He laughed. "Just thought we'd take it easy tonight. Besides, your dad wouldn't take too kindly to me if I were serving his daughter any other kind of beverage while on a date."

Date? Hannah felt her heart quicken. Feeling almost punch-drunk with pleasure, she pulled out the box of chocolates. "This is it?" She asked, holding each in a hand. Josh laughed as he lay back on the blanket. "That's it. It's too late for dinner, so I thought I'd bring dessert."

"Actually..." she said slowly. "Good idea. What's dinner without dessert?"

"My sentiments exactly," Josh said, sitting up a bit, and resting on his elbow. He relieved her of the box of chocolates. "If you aren't going to open them," he said, removing the lid, "I will."

Laughing, Hannah sat next to Josh. It felt good to be outside in the fresh air after a week in the stuffy house. She felt as though her head had finally cleared, despite the unsightly bump that still showcased eight stitches.

Josh held a chocolate out to her, and as she moved to take it, he slowly shook his head. Blinking, she held her breath as he gently slid the butter crème past her lips. *Why am I blushing?* Hannah wondered as the candy began to melt in her mouth.

If Josh had seen her cheeks go all rosy-red, he gave no sign of it. Smiling, he lay on his back and tucked his hands under his head. "Remember when we used to do this at the river? We'd swim, look up at the stars, sometimes, we'd camp out all night."

Hannah rolled onto her back beside him, gazing through wind-shifted leaves at the stars beyond. "Yeah," she sighed, "back in the days, when we had our whole lives to look forward to."

Josh rolled onto his side, propped his head on his palm. "We still have our whole lives to look forward to." And tucking a tendril of hair behind her ear, he added, "We're only twenty-three."

She forced herself to look back up at the sky. "How can anyone who's only twenty-three have made so many mistakes?"

"You made one mistake, Hannah. Just one. If falling for the wrong person was a crime, the jails would be over-run with people."

Hannah shifted so she could stare into his eyes. "All I can say is, thank God for second chances."

His eyes glittered and glimmered, reflecting the light of a million stars. Josh swallowed, then sat up and pulled two wine glasses from the picnic basket, and opening the bottle of Cabernet, he filled each halfway and held one out to her. When she sat up to take it, he clinked his glass to hers. "To new beginnings."

There was something different about him tonight, Hannah noted. She owed it to him to at least try and understand him as well as he understood her. "To new beginnings," she echoed.

They sipped and their eyes met over the rims of the goblets. Hannah knew then, deep down that she was in love with Josh. And judging by the look on his face, he felt the same. It warmed her all the way down to her toes, made them tingle, made her heart quicken, and her palms sweat. She loved the way it felt, being in love with her best friend. It was freeing and comfortable, safe and overwhelming all at once.

Realizing too much time had passed in this strange and almost-awkward silence, Hannah said, "Mmm. This stuff is good. Can I get some more?"

"Yeah." He held the bottle up. She put out her glass, watching as some sloshed over the rim.

Josh screwed the cap on. "Okay," he challenged, "now it's your turn to toast."

There were so many things she'd like to say. Here's to being in love again. Here's to a lifetime spent with you. "Oh, okay... hmm," she thought for a second, deciding to keep the moment light. "Here's to the many, many dates you've enjoyed over the years," Hannah said, referring to the few he did have. She brought the glass to her lips, trying not to laugh.

Josh pretended to choke on his drink. "Hey...." And after taking another sip, he held up his glass. "And here's to being twenty-three and still living with your dad."

Hannah giggled. "To your freshman year of college."

"What! That's not nice," Josh sputtered playfully. Then, recovering, he sat up, clearly enjoying himself.

"Okay, okay... to graduating college with a broken hand," he said, raising his glass triumphantly in the air.

"Mmm-hmm, your dad told me that story."

Still laughing, Hannah was having a difficult time taking a drink. She calmed herself enough to say, "Here's to your college degree in business," before another onslaught of giggles attacked again.

"Here's to yours," Josh countered. "And your many job prospects."

Soon, Hannah was laughing so hard that tears ran down her cheeks and her sides ached. She could barely coax the next toast past her lips. "And here's to you," she stammered around giggles, "to you and... Emma—"

"Okay, that does it!" Josh grinned, and tossing his glass aside, he tackled her.

Squealing, she dropped her own when he pinned her arms to the ground. Hannah squirmed and laughed but quickly realized that she was helplessly pinned beneath him. Josh seemed to realize the same thing. Their laughter slowly subsided and their smiles faded, until all that was left between them was the heat from their bodies pressed together. Desire emanated from Josh's eyes as his breathing fell into rhythm with hers, and she reveled at how perfectly they seemed to fit together. They heard a loud hiss and froze, looking around in confusion. A split second later, sprinklers shot spouts of water out of the ground, soaking them.

They scrambled to their feet, grabbing what they could and tripping over one another as they dashed through the spraying water, getting soaked. By the time they reached dry land, they were drenched to the skin. They leaned breathlessly against Josh's car, the soggy blanket hanging from his hand and Hannah gripping the basket in front of her to cover her clinging pink shirt. Her hair was drenched and stuck to her face, sending driblets of water trickling down her neck and onto her chest. The moonlight caught them and made her skin pucker and gleam in the cool breeze.

"That backfired if I do say so myself," Josh said,

running a hand through his wet hair.

Hannah shivered beside him. "Yeah. That was unexpected."

They looked at each other and laughed. Josh opened the trunk, tossing the blanket inside. Then he reached for the picnic basket, but Hannah kept a firm hold on it. "What...?" Josh's eyes flickered to her chest. He looked away quickly, embarrassed. "Oh... yeah." He fumbled for his keys, unlocked the door and withdrew a towel. He tossed it at her.

"Thanks." Hannah wrapped it around her, feeling slightly warmer, and put the basket in his trunk.

They climbed stiffly into his car and Josh turned it on quickly to get some warm air circulating.

"Did you have anything else planned for tonight?" Hannah teased as they drove away.

Josh laughed. "You're just full of jokes tonight, aren't you?"

They're laughter dwindled, leaving a comfortable silence between them. Hannah watched the quiet darkness whirring past the windows and felt at peace for the first time in a week. As this feeling settled on her, Hannah began to see things about her town she'd never noticed before. Buildings she never paid any attention to before that now looked like home. Houses with porch lights burning, trees that had grown in front yards for generations. Cars parked in driveways as families gathered in their dens. Churches of all denominations, each with stately steeples that welcome those spiritually oppressed. Not so long ago, she hated this place and everything in it. Now she realized that she did love Linbeck after all, in part thanks to Josh, who with his gestures taught her that second chances really are possible.

He left the car running after pulling into her driveway as Hannah gathered up her flowers, which had wilted a little from the heat. The slight crumpled edges of the petals made her somewhat sad, and she felt anxious to get them in water.

When the radio DJ announced the next tune, Hannah had no trouble admitting what a wonderful time she had. Plucking at her wet shirt, she tacked on a playful, "Despite the unexpected shower."

"Me too," he chuckled.

Gingerly holding her flowers, she met his eyes. "Thanks for being so good to me," she said quietly.

He searched her face, no doubt waiting for her characteristic sarcastic remark. When none came, a slow smile spread across his face. "I am the only friend you have."

Giggling quietly, she took a deep breath. Someday, she'd prove to him exactly how much she cherished that friendship. Now the DJ announced it was nine o'clock. Hannah didn't want to get out of the car. Didn't want the evening to end. Didn't want to leave him. "So," she said, procrastinating, "you have plans for the rest of the night?"

"Nope." Cocking his head slightly, he wiggled his eyebrows. "Why...?"

"You could grab that picnic basket and we can finish the Cabernet and those chocolates in front of a good *Lifetime* movie." It was Hannah's turn to wiggle her eyebrows.

Without a word, Josh turned off the ignition. "How about we see if there's a good baseball game on, instead?" And in the companionable silence that bloomed as they headed for her front door, something told Hannah that Josh was back to his old self – the one that wanted to be more than just friends.

~ EIGHT ~

Summer was slipping away. The days were getting shorter, the nights cooler, and fall was already evident in the slowly changing leaves. With autumn approaching, Linbeck's annual Summer Farewell Picnic celebrated its arrival. Local businesses, churches, and residents participated in the affair, setting up food and craft booths, live music, and displays. The highlight of the event was a fireworks show at dusk over Linbeck Lake. Hannah had attended the event since she could remember, usually as a spectator. This year, however, she'd volunteered to help with set up through her dad's church. If there were ever a time to turn over a new leaf, this was the perfect opportunity.

The past week she'd dedicated most of her time to gathering decorations, painting signs for booths, and baking mass amounts of Butter Horn Nut Rolls, Derby Pies, Ginger Snaps, and Thumbprint cookies with the girls at the church. Now, Hannah straightened the last checkered tablecloth on the picnic table and looked around the park with satisfaction.

An endless blue sky stretched over Linbeck, promising a perfect day as a cool breeze gently ruffled the crepe paper streamers and banners posted at the booths. People had already started drifting in, those hesitant to leave summer behind still in shorts, but most in jeans and light jackets. The smell of grills being fired up mingled with the scent of fresh cut grass.

"Hey hon," her father said as he placed an affectionate arm around her shoulders. "Everything looks great. Thanks for all the help."

Hannah smiled at him and leaned her head on his shoulder. "I enjoyed it. I had more fun than I have in a long time."

He squeezed her arm, looking out over the park. "I've seen a much happier side of you the past few weeks. You've been a blessing to the church and the homeless

103

shelter for all the help you've been giving. And I know Josh and the youth group are thankful, too." Michael glanced at her. "You sure you're okay, though? You've been going an awful lot lately, not sleeping or eating much—"

"Dad," Hannah interrupted. "Thanks for your concern, but I'm fine. Really. I'm glad I can finally give back to you and Josh, after all you've done for me."

With the miscarriage behind her and a hole in her heart, she'd done a lot of soul searching. Hannah didn't like who she'd become. Didn't like the fact that she was becoming her mother more with each passing day. It was from a selfish woman who no longer wanted the life she'd chosen that had caused Hannah and her dad more pain than imaginable. And Hannah refused to walk in those footsteps.

Michael gave her another squeeze before dropping his arm. "You're my daughter. I'd do anything for you."

Hannah felt her heart overflow with his love that was so absolute and unconditional. How could she have ever treated him so badly? How could she have been so blinded with anger at her mother and Ben that she hadn't seen how he'd continued to love her, despite her bad attitude and mistakes?

"Dad," Hannah said, trying to hide the overwhelming emotion in her voice. "I'm so sorry for all the years of... of worry I've caused. And for being disrespectful and unthankful for what you've given me."

Michael smiled down at her. "Worry and fear comes with the job." He shrugged. "As for the rest? I forgave you a long time ago, sweetheart."

Hannah swiped at a wayward tear. "Thanks, Dad." Hannah thought of the thousands of little things he'd done over the years, never complaining, never keeping lists, like helping her with homework and dropping her off to see a movie with her friends. "And thanks for always being one of the few people I could always count on."

"I love you," he said again. "It was worth a little heart-ache to see the young woman you've become." Then he laughed. "Let's save the seriousness for later." He gathered Hannah in a tight hug and kissed her forehead. "Duty calls. Have fun." Michael waved at someone in the distance and headed in their direction.

Hannah watched him for a second, a smile lingering on her face.

"Hey Baby," Josh said, interrupting her thoughts. He hefted a blue Coleman cooler onto the bench of the picnic table.

"Hey." Hannah turned to him, her eyes drawn to his muscular arms in his T-shirt.

Josh nodded in the direction of the booths and other picnic tables as he opened the cooler. "Looks like all your hard work paid off. Everything looks good."

"Thanks," she said, stepping forward to adjust the tablecloth that kept blowing up in the determined autumn breeze. "What's in there?"

"Ahhh." With precision and care, Josh withdrew a baking pan of marinating meat. "Mrs. Austin's barbeque ribs."

Hannah gasped and stepped forward to inspect the contents of the pan. "Her prize-winning ribs? And she's trusting you with them?"

Josh inhaled deeply. "Yep and yep. Since I'm the head chef at our booth, she's put her ribs in my tender loving care."

"Aren't you special."

He winked and placed them back in the cooler. "That seems to be the consensus." Josh grabbed the cooler and started towards their booth. "C'mon. I have to get these on the grill."

Hannah followed him, waving at familiar faces as they went. The grounds were now bustling with activity. The aromatic scent of cooking meat and fresh desserts filled the air as the sound of laughter, mingling voices, and music got louder.

"Hey Hannah! How are you?" Erin asked as she approach-ed, her arms loaded down with the goodies they'd all baked.

"Oh, let me help you," Hannah said, rushing to her side and relieving her of a few pans.

"I've been so excited for this all week," Erin said, her eyes bright.

"Me, too," Hannah admitted, peeling the cover off a pan of cookies. "It's always been something I looked forward to, even when I was little."

Erin bit into a cookie and giggled. "Oh yeah, I remember all the fun we used to have. Like the year we got lost in the woods trying to find the best spot to watch the fireworks. Our parents flipped out and had half the town out looking for us."

Hannah laughed while she slid each cookie on small squares of wax paper. "Yeah. Good times, especially getting grounded for a week."

A few other girls from the church showed up and began helping arrange the rest of the desserts. The afternoon sped by as they talked about past years at the picnics and other church events and before Hannah knew it, her stomach was rumbling and her legs ached.

She peered over Josh's shoulder at the loaded grill. "Smells great. Think I could get a hot dog?"

He wiped his brow with the back of his hand and grinned at her. "No ribs for the lady?"

"While I would love some, Mrs. Austin made them for the picnic guests. But a hot dog would be great."

"Have a seat. This batch will be done in a second."

A few minutes later, Josh approached her carrying a paper plate with two hot dogs and a bag of Lays potato chips. He sat beside her and tore open the bag, offering them to her.

"Thank you." Hannah grabbed a handful. "Break time?"

Josh leaned back and put his elbows on the table behind him. "Yeah, Sean is taking over for a while," he said, nodding toward Erin's husband.

Hannah nibbled on a chip. "Can you believe summer is almost over?"

"It went fast this year," Josh agreed.

"Yeah." Hannah slid the rest of the chip in her mouth and dusted greasy salt from her fingertips. "Seems like last week it was just starting."

"You've had me running crazy the past few months. I haven't had a chance to slow down and breath."

Smiling, Hannah grabbed her hot dog and took a bite. "Oh, quit complaining. You've had as much fun as I have," she said around a mouthful.

He shook his head as he drew a thin line of ketchup onto his hot dog. "I thought for a while you were going to replace me with all the new friends you made at the homeless shelter."

"While I'm beginning to find Jerry awfully cute, there still isn't anyone who can replace you." Most Sunday afternoons found them at the Allen County Homeless Shelter, a place that, (just a few months ago), Hannah thought she'd never return. She recalled that first trip, when the sights and odors of the place had turned her stomach. But after making it a point to go a second time, compassion had filled her instead. She saw a bit of herself in the unkempt poor passing through: lost, lonely, searching. Now, the smells no longer made her sick, and the people knew her by name. She'd become friends with other volunteers, and Jerry, the cook, teasingly asked her out every time she showed up.

"So, maybe this could be a new career for you? Manager of a homeless facility?" Josh teased as he loaded his plate with chips.

"Hmm, no," Hannah said thoughtfully. While she enjoyed it during her off time, her career interests lay solely in journalism. Still, she couldn't resist messing with Josh. "I'd rather be a football coach," she said.

Josh snorted, almost choking on the bite of hot dog

in his mouth. "Right. My team didn't just beat yours, they annihilated you."

Hannah couldn't help but laugh. "The look on your face when I sacked you was worth the effort."

"You're a cheater. First of all, I'd called a time out." Josh jumped to his feet, pointing his finger in her face.

She swatted it away and shook her head, barely containing her laughter.

"No one heard it. This so called 'time-out' of yours is a cover-up for being tackled by a girl!"

Clearly enjoying their banter, Josh's face lit up. "Oh, c'mon. So you didn't hear your entire team yelling 'stop'?"

Hannah stared at him, giving him a moment to calm down while she fought the urge to smile. "Are you done?"

He waved his hand at her in exasperation and reclaimed his seat on the picnic table. "Yeah I'm done. And you're done coaching my youth group."

"Don't get nasty." Hannah nudged him with her shoulder, emitting a smile from him. "Fine, no more football. But you can't keep me away from summer camp."

He shooed a fly from his meal. "I don't think your fan club would let me keep you away. The girls followed you around like lost little puppies the entire weekend."

Hannah stole a chip from his plate and slid it into her mouth. "You're upset about the fireflies in your bed." She hid a giggle.

Josh chuckled with satisfaction. "It didn't beat the blow horn at two in the morning and watching all of you fall out of your beds."

"I think the best part of that weekend was the last night," Hannah said, looking at her fingers and blushing.

Josh's laughter subsided as he glanced at her. He looked at his empty plate, then back at her, suddenly seeming uncomfortable.

"Hey, Mister Reynolds." A little boy from the youth

group bounded up to them, his red hair ruffled from the wind and his cheeks rosy. "Can I have a hot dog? My mom told me to ask you."

"Sure, Jared." Josh got to his feet and started toward the grill. "Right over here." He looked at Hannah over his shoulder. "Be right back."

She nodded, her heart feeling heavy. His reaction wasn't what she'd hoped for. After a week at summer camp with the youth group and no time alone, Hannah had decided to surprise Josh with a fire and S'mores on the final night. She'd crept out of her cot after the entire camp was asleep and built a fire in the pit. Under the moonlight, Hannah had gathered pebbles and tossed them at his window until she saw his shadow in the window.

"Hannah? What are you doing?" He'd hissed through the screen.

"Come here. I have something to show you!"

A few moments passed and Hannah feared Josh wasn't going to show, leaving her standing alone in the darkness like a fool. But then she heard the hinges on his cabin door whine in protest as he snuck out to meet her.

Hannah recalled how delighted he'd been at her surprise, and they'd spent most of the night talking about nothing in particular, laughing and stuffing themselves with chocolate and marshmallows in front of the glowing fire. Then, as they returned to their cabins she'd turned to him, thinking she'd hug him goodnight or kiss him on the cheek. As she leaned in, Josh apparently misread her closeness. Her cheek touched his and then he turned, either to reciprocate or to get away, Hannah didn't know. Either way, the result was that her mouth touched Josh's. Surprised, she started to pull back until he put a purposeful hand on the back of her neck and pulled her lips once again to his.

But almost as soon as it began, it ended when Josh pulled away, looking elated, ashamed, and confused all at once. "I should get back." Then he'd stepped around her and disappeared into the darkness of his cabin, leaving her dizzy and breathless in the moonlight.

Now, Hannah watched as Josh tended to Jared, his manner so tender and caring. She could tell she'd hit on a sensitive topic, but that night two weeks ago had sent her reeling with a thousand questions that had since gone unaddressed.

As soon as Jared had his hot dog and bounced back into the crowd, Josh returned his attention to her. He wiped his hands on a towel and walked back to the picnic table, sitting beside her in silence. "About that night..." Josh began uncomfortably. "I... I was out of line. You're going through a lot right now and—"

"If you regret it, tell me," Hannah said softly. "Don't make up excuses."

He sighed and set his plate down beside him. "I don't regret it. I just want to give you time to recover from what happened," he explained slowly.

"I didn't lose my mind, Josh. I—"

"Lost a baby," he finished for her, looking her square in the eyes. "That's a big thing. And more than enough right now."

Hannah looked at her hands, knowing he was right. She'd struggled with losing the baby. She couldn't even count the hours she'd spent on her knees praying to God to help her find the strength and courage to move on. Still, weeks later, Hannah had moments where longing and regret filled her heart and made it hard to breathe. But the new plan she had for her life made it all a little easier and she was slowly finding ways to get past the pain.

"It's hard for you to understand," Hannah said softly. "But I'm trying to move on. I need to move on."

Josh's face softened but he didn't seem convinced. "I understand. But you need time to heal—not just from the baby, but from Ben, too."

"Hey Josh! Hey Hannah!" A few of the teens from the youth group walked by, heading toward the volleyball nets and waved.

Hannah forced what she hoped was a cheerful smile and noticed Josh's tight grin. As soon as the kids passed, the uncomfortable air returned. In an attempt to change the conversation to lighter subjects, Hannah asked, "What are you doing next weekend?"

"Uh oh," Josh said, looking relieved to be momentarily let off the hook. "I recognize that tone. That's your 'I want to go skydiving' or 'let's bungee jump' tone." He shook his head and chuckled. "What do you have in mind this time?"

"A hot air balloon ride," she said, feeling her cheeks redden at the fact that Josh knew her so well. She hadn't figured out where to get the money for such an adventure, considering she was still jobless. It had sounded fun at the time she was entertaining the idea.

Concern was written all over his face, making Hannah feel guilty. She hadn't meant to worry anyone with her yearnings for excitement. In the past it had been a way for her to escape her hurt and anger, and she was now realizing she had some old habits that needed attention.

"You're crazy," Josh told her. "You know that, right? You've been going and going, barely sleeping or eating - you look like you've lost ten pounds. It goes well with the bags under your eyes." He popped a chip into his mouth and then pointed toward her eyes, as if to make his point.

Hannah glanced at him. His apprehension overwhelmed her, made her feel warm inside. Despite his apparent regret for having kissed her, at least he still cared. Still, she couldn't help but wonder why he regretted that kiss. Maybe, as he'd said, it was because of concern for her health, and that she still loved Ben. But Hannah couldn't shake the fear that it was more - that perhaps Josh's feelings for her had never been romantic, that he'd been blinded by the moment and now realized his mistake. That possibility made her heart sink to her stomach.

A wayward volleyball suddenly rolled toward their table. One of the teens that passed them began to jog over to retrieve it, but Josh got up and grabbed it, tossing it to the young man. As Hannah watched, she decided to give her worries to God, trusting that He would take care of her. If Josh wasn't in God's plan for her future, she didn't want to pursue it. Hannah had taken her own path one too many times, and had finally learned from her mistakes.

Michael approached them, doing his best to unruffle his windblown hair. Hannah noted his lean frame and how, without his reading glasses, he looked young and happy.

"Hey kids," he said, waving. "You two planning to stick around for the fireworks?"

"Of course," Hannah replied. The fireworks were the main event at the picnic and there was no way anyone in town would miss them.

"We're going to watch from the lake," Josh told him.

Michael shielded his eyes from the sun. "Better get a spot soon, then. It's filling up fast." His attention turned to someone behind them and he waved. "Sorry, kids. I need to take care of a few things." With a wink, he started back through the crowd. "Save me a spot!" He called over his shoulder.

"Guess we'd better go stake out some lawn," Hannah said to Josh.

He got to his feet. "That's already been taken care of."

"Really?" Hannah stood up. "All these years looking for the best seat, and you've finally found it?"

Josh grinned as they headed toward the booth to help close it down. "I happened on it while I was fishing one day about two years ago. Only a few others have found it."

Already, the sun was getting low in the sky and with dusk came a cooler breeze that swept through the grounds. Booths began closing up as people filtered out of the park, leaving the lingering feeling of another day winding down.

Hannah helped Erin package the last of the desserts

while Josh and a few others loaded the grill and leftover meat in the church's van. After everything was clean, the remaining few people trickled off into the quickly descending darkness to wait for the fireworks to begin.

Tucking the last sign into the already overstuffed van, Hannah turned and saw Josh patiently waiting for her, a sweatshirt slung over his shoulder.

"Ready?" he asked, holding out his hand.

Nodding, Hannah slid hers into it and let him lead her, feeling the cool wind nipping at her bare arms. Wishing she'd remembered a sweater, she shivered. There wasn't any time to get a blanket, let alone a jacket, so she followed Josh without a word.

Tucked in the back of the park was a narrow, inconspicuous trail that led to a small, white sand beach on the edge of the lake. A few other people had discovered the same place, but other than them, they were alone. As dusk swept through, a few boats dotted the jetty so that by the time the darkness fully enveloped them, their blinking lights were chasing the shadows away. Linbeck Lake was small enough to see the opposite shore where a row of cottages sat nestled in the Weeping Willows, the lights from their windows glowing in the nearly complete darkness.

As they stood on the strip of beach, Hannah slid off her shoes, digging her toes in the cool sand. After the long day on her feet, being barefoot was a welcome relief. Following suit, Josh stripped his shoes and socks off, too, and settled on the ground.

The lapping water sucked at the shore as the breeze carried an expectant murmur from the waiting people. In the distance, Hannah heard the squeal of children playing and saw the fiery flashes of their sparklers.

Hannah was enjoying the comfortable silence between Josh and she, feeling there was nothing to say that could make the moment any better. As the first firework finally burst through the darkness, changing the sky from its inky blackness to a rainbow of vibrant, sparkling lights that rained high above them, Josh gave her his sweater. Hannah accepted it with a smile, wanting to reach for him, to kiss him. Most of all, she wanted to tell the world she had fallen completely in love with him. Instead, she slid her hand in his, feeling a twinge of regret that she couldn't tell him, tell the world, how wonderful it was to be in love with her best friend.

~ * ~

Editorial Assistant. Hannah circled the ad and brought the pen thoughtfully to her lips. This job was exactly what she needed. It would pay enough to get her a small apartment and on her own two feet.

She went in search of the resume she'd started months earlier and found it haphazardly tucked into a folder at the bottom of her still full school bag. For the rest of the afternoon, Hannah carefully perfected it until she was satisfied and then put it in the mailbox with a wistful prayer. Within a week she got the call for an interview the following day.

~ * ~

Hannah posed and smoothed her skirt. "How do I look?" she asked her dad, adjusting her collar.

Her father looked up from the newspaper and gave the thumbs-up sign. "Great, sweetheart."

"Dad," she breathed, pacing, "I'm so nervous. What if I don't get the job?"

"You'll get it, but even if you don't," he said, shrugging, "you'll apply for another."

"What if they hate me?"

"How could anyone hate you?"

"But what if—"

"Honey," he interrupted gently, "calm down." He laid the paper across his lap. "You're well prepared. You have an excellent resume. What's not to like?"

She smiled fleetingly, then caught sight of the clock. "Oh my goodness. I have to go." Hastily, she grabbed her purse.

Following her gaze, he frowned. "I thought the interview was at three."

"It is. But it's one-thirty." She headed into the foyer. "Wouldn't want to be late. Terrible first impress—"

"It only takes twenty minutes to get to Allen County."

"There might be traffic." Tapping her watch, Hannah added, "I read that when job candidates arrive early, it shows prospective employers initiative."

He held up his hands in mock surrender. "Never hurts to be early," he said, grinning.

"Bye, Dad. Say a prayer for me, will you?" she called over her shoulder. As she hurried down the walk, Hannah realized her stomach was doing somersaults. Her hands felt clammy as she dug keys from her purse, and her foot was heavy on the gas as she backed out of the drive. At the stop sign on the corner, Hannah took a deep breath and asked God to ease her spirit. This interview was the first page of her new life—*Chapter One* in the career she longed for.

A honk from the car behind her brought her back to reality. With a polite wave of apology, she headed toward town, realizing her dad was right. It'd only taken twenty minutes to get there.

Calmed by her dad's encouraging words and her moments with God, Hannah entered the building. It seemed to take the elevator forever to arrive. Alone in the tiny car, she smoothed her blouse and tucked her hair behind her ears, leaned closer to the chromed button panel to check her lipstick, and lurched with fright as the doors chimed open.

A set of cherry wood double doors at the end of the hallway greeted her. On the glass panes Allen County News was written in neat, white letters. Hannah read it as she approached, then grasped the knob, and after lifting her chin, entered. She was shocked to see six other people seated in the waiting room. Heart thumping with anticipation and dread, Hannah scooted between the glass and chrome coffee table to take the last available chair. She leafed through a tattered issue of the paper, trying her best to look nonchalant, as if she didn't even notice every tick of the clock.

A middle aged woman, her dark brown hair pinned tightly at the nape of her neck and a pair of tortoise shell glasses balanced on her nose, opened a door labeled 'employees only.' Every eye turned to her as she glanced at the clipboard in her hand. "Tanya Bolling," the woman called out, her eyes skimming the waiting room.

A girl dressed in a gray pantsuit one size too big got to her feet and awkwardly made her way to the woman who introduced herself as Monica. Judging by the deer-in-the-headlight look in the girl's eyes, Hannah guessed she was fresh out of college and this was one of her first interviews. Taking stock of her own nervousness, Hannah said a little prayer for the young woman.

As the minutes stretched on, Hannah found herself staring blankly at the newspaper in front of her, her mind miles away. She wondered about the people beside her. Were they more experienced? More talented? Better at interviewing? Glancing at her watch, she saw that Tanya's interview had run over into Hannah's appointed time. This fact made her stomach twist with anticipation that perhaps the job was already filled by the scared, awkward girl.

She glanced at the six remaining people, wondering if they were in situations like her own, where money was nonexistent, still living with their parents. Aside from that, Hannah wanted to earn her own way and do something productive. She'd always felt, even as a little girl, that writing was one of the best ways to reach people. Here was her chance.

Just as Hannah had nearly convinced herself that Tanya was probably setting up her own office in the back, the door swung open and Monica stepped out, looking just as prim as she had thirty minutes earlier.

"Hannah Sinclair."

Feeling all eyes on her, Hannah took a deep breath and joined Monica in the front of the room.

"Hi Hannah. I'm Monica," she said after a brief handshake. "Follow me and we'll get started."

Hannah smiled cheerfully, trying to appear confident, all the while praying that God would be with her. When they reached the conference room, Monica motioned for her to take a seat at the table. Hannah sat, watching as Monica reviewed her resume attached to the clipboard.

"Hmm," she mumbled, her finger skimming each line. "I see you graduated with honors, and you have some excellent credentials."

Finally, Monica leaned back in her chair. Legs crossed, pen in hand, she seemed so serious in all aspects of the word that Hannah felt herself fidgeting under her scrutiny. "Tell me about yourself, Hannah."

She'd been prepared for this question. After a couple hours researching interviewing techniques, Hannah had compiled a complete list of questions, answers, to-dos, and don't-dos. She felt herself relax as she recited what she'd practiced, and most of the questions that followed were just as easy. Other than the dreaded, "What is one of your weaknesses?" curveball and a, "What would you do in this or that situation?", Hannah felt things were going reasonably well. After asking if Hannah had any questions, Monica turned to the resume, causing a silence so loud Hannah could hear her pulse thundering in her ears.

Monica folded both hands on the conference table and leaned forward to meet Hannah's eyes. "You seem to be what we're looking for but we can't make a decision we've completed all the interviews. You can expect to hear one way or another by tomorrow afternoon."

With that, Monica stood and shook Hannah's hand, putting the interview to a close. As Hannah headed down the hall and out the double doors, she felt a bit of angst and a bit of relief. The interview was over, (thank the

Lord), but how on earth she was going to keep herself from staring at the phone until tomorrow afternoon was beyond her.

~ * ~

Hannah was wiping the last dish dry when the phone rang. Dropping it back into the sudsy water, she raced to the living room, nearly colliding with her father as he was reaching for the cordless system.

She grinned as he put his hands on his hips. "This is Hannah," she said into the receiver.

The familiar voice on the other line caused her to stop in her tracks. Hannah faced her dad as she listened, trying not to react as he mouthed 'is that her?' Smiling, she paced, nodded, and bit her lower lip to keep from shouting into Monica's ear.

"Mmm-hmm. Okay, thank you," Hannah said, then hung up.

"Well?" her dad asked.

She did a little jig around the living room. "I got it!" Hannah squealed, hopping up and down. "I got it!"

"When do you start?" His face lit up with delight.

"Next Monday." Then, she grabbed the phone. "I've got to tell Josh. I promised to call him the minute I heard."

Pulling his keys from his pocket, he nodded. "I need to get back to work anyway," he said, giving her a warm hug and a peck on the cheek. "Congratulations, sweetie. See you at suppertime."

Hannah sent him a half-hearted wave and put the phone back into its cradle. No answer on Josh's cell. Her gaze fell upon the morning paper, folded neatly on the kitchen counter. She grabbed it and flipped to the real estate section. "Time to do a little apartment hunting."

Despite its size, the Linbeck paper boasted two columns of ads for apartments within her price range. Circling each, she phoned a few and narrowed her search to two ideal units. As she was wrapping up the final call, the doorbell rang.

At the sound of Josh's familiar "Hello!" Hannah poked her head into the hall and waved him inside. "Okay," she said into the phone when he entered the kitchen, "I'll try and stop by later today. Thanks."

Josh helped himself to a glass of iced tea. "Is your dad around? I have a couple things from work I need to talk to him about."

"He just went back." Hannah couldn't contain her excitement. "You're looking at the new Editorial Assistant of Allen County Times," she said, spreading her hands out elaborately. "I start next Monday."

"You got it?" Josh swung her into his arms, squeezing her tightly.

"I'm going apartment shopping the rest of the week," Hannah told him, her voice muffled in his chest.

"So it's true. You're actually sticking around Linbeck this time?" Josh asked, pulling slightly away so he could see her.

Hannah saw the hope in his eyes, and her heart skipped a beat. "Looks like it," she told him. She didn't mention that he was the main reason she was staying.

He smiled down at her, revealing his dimple. "Good."

Hannah stood under his gaze, her body still pressed against his. The familiarity of it made the heat move through her. Josh searched her face, his eyes tender. Hannah waited, thinking, hoping, he was going to kiss her. But then Josh suddenly stepped back. He cleared his throat and tucked his hands in his pockets.

"Congratulations. I'm happy for you."

Remembering what he'd said at the picnic about giving her time to heal, Hannah swallowed a sigh and managed to smile. "Thanks."

"I have to get going." He looked at her, something unrecognizable in his eyes, then started for the door.

Hannah accompanied Josh to his car where he opened the door and turned to her. "Let me know if you need help with apartment hunting," he said.

She wished he would talk to her about the static be-tween them, wished for once he would stop trying to pro-tect her and tell her how he felt about her but her own courage to confront Josh had all but diminished. Instead, she just waved as he got in his car.

Her heart sank with disappointment when he backed out of the drive. Every time she thought he was falling for her, something happened to make her second-guess it. They had been best friends since they were five, and grew apart because of her selfishness. Now it seemed that every time she made an attempt to get that closeness back, Josh distanced himself.

Hannah knew it was because of her past, and she couldn't blame him. After all, she hadn't exactly been the greatest friend in recent years, or up front with him when she'd returned from those years of silence. Even so, it made her feel heavy with regret that she hadn't taken bet-ter care of the friendship God had blessed her with.

Sighing, Hannah headed back inside, thinking how good pork chops sounded for supper. Being one of her dad's favorite meals, she figured it would help her break the news that she intended to move out when she'd saved enough money for the deposit and first month's rent.

Maybe her dad would try to talk her out of moving and maybe she'd let him, for now.

Perhaps that would give her time to try and prove to her dad she was changing after all. And prove to Josh he could trust her again. Then again, maybe being on her own and making her own way in the world would be enough proof for the both of them.

While Hannah started supper, she prayed it wasn't too late to fix everything she'd broken.

~ NINE ~

Apartment shopping proved to be less than exciting. It gave Hannah a headache and most days she was discouraged by what she saw. After two weeks, she finally threw her hands in the air and settled on a small one-bedroom unit with a tiny porch that overlooked the carport. A few plants and pictures and it would look good enough, she figured. It was, after all, a place to call her own.

Being on her own also meant she would no longer have the convenience of using her father's car. After the two of them did some searching, Michael found an elderly couple at the church who were selling their '91 Camry at a decent price. Finally, Hannah felt her life slowly piecing together as she drove out to meet her dad at his house. He seemed somewhat downtrodden as he helped her pack her few things for the move. She knew he enjoyed her presence in the house again after so many years of being alone.

"Dad, cheer up," Hannah said lightly, nudging him with her elbow as she passed. "I'm only ten minutes away."

He smiled, his eyes looking sad as he heaved a loaded laundry basket from the trunk of his car. "It's never easy to let go," he said. "I'll never stop worrying about you no matter how close you are."

Josh helped her track down some decent furniture from garage sales and as she slowly began settling in, she realized her place looked like a thrift shop. Mismatched and worn chairs, coffee tables, and dressers were scattered in each room. With the walls a bleak, stark white, Hannah saw she had a lot of work ahead of her if she wanted to feel at home. Her exasperation diminished a little after realizing it could be an excuse to use Josh's handyman skills.

"You free tonight?" Hannah asked Josh over the phone one morning. "Don't worry, no bungee jumping is involved."

"Then what is involved?"

Was it her imagination, or did he sound suggestive? "Just some sanding. Maybe a little staining. I need to fix this place up."

"Your landlord is okay with it?"

Hannah looked at the dresser with dismay. "Not the apartment – the furniture. Some of it's so beat up it's about to fall apart." She could almost see his adorable grin.

"I guess I could squeeze it in my schedule," he teased. "How about six?"

"Perfect. See you then," she said, feeling a little smug that she'd found the perfect excuse to spend an evening with him.

By late morning, the sky had turned cloudy and dark. Streaks of lightening zapped across the distance and the air was moist with the threat of rain. Hannah hurried to the hardware store to purchase supplies and get the last of the stain she needed before the clouds opened up.

This kind of weather always terrified and thrilled her. She could recall a couple instances when she and her dad huddled in the basement watching the trees lash at the tiny window above their heads as the tornado siren blared in the distance. Now, with the impending danger of a bad storm ahead, Hannah felt grateful for all the times her father had made her feel safe. It made her miss him, though, and she made a mental note to call him when her project was finished.

Hannah turned on the news while she moved the dresser away from the wall and covered the floor around it with plastic sheeting. By three, the rain arrived with boiling clouds that looked threatening. An insistent beeping from the television informed her of a tornado watch.

Hannah nervously paced in her living room, glancing from the TV to the window, as if one would disagree with the other. A few minutes later, the phone rang.

"Hey!" Josh said loudly from the other end. "I got off work early because of the weather. I'm coming over now."

Relieved, Hannah hung up, noticing the eerie green color of the sky. It wasn't looking good, she thought.

Josh burst in after a brief knock on her door. A sea of wind and rain followed him, and Hannah could smell the electric odor in the air.

"Wow," he said breathlessly, shedding his drenched coat. "It's really coming down out there."

"Tornado warning," Hannah said pointing at the TV.

As she hung up his coat, Josh eyed her. "You scared?"

She glanced out the window, then at him. "Yeah. Aren't you?"

He laughed and pocketed his hands, pausing in the bedroom doorway. "You've been a Midwesterner long enough to know it'll pass soon, so don't worry." He walked the perimeter of the room, assessing the furniture. When he faced her, he rubbed his palms together. "What are we fixing? The dresser and...?"

Hannah pointed. "The nightstand. And the coffee table if we have time."

He nodded. "Ready to do this? Shouldn't take too long with both of us working."

Hannah stooped to pry the lid from a can of oak finish. "If you think you're leaving before this weather clears," she said, shaking the screwdriver at him, "you're not."

He stooped and grabbed the sandpaper. "I wasn't planning on it," he said, a slight smile on his lips.

Feeling a little safer with Josh nearby, Hannah stirred the coffee-colored liquid. The truth behind his statement warmed her but at the same time made her realize how different they'd turned out. Swallowing heavily, she felt the guilt resurface again, a reminder of how she'd abandoned him and her father.

Making a conscious decision not to reply, she changed the subject instead. "I won't be buying new furniture anytime soon," she said as she dipped the brush into the can. "Not after all this."

"Whoa, whoa." Josh brushed her hand away before the stain touched the wood. "First we sand. Then we paint."

"Oh." Balancing the brush over the opening of the can, she found a sanding block. "You must do this a lot."

Josh worked fast covering nearly half the side in the same amount of time it took her to do a quarter of it. "Here and there. Sometimes it's cheaper to salvage a piece rather than replace it with a new one."

"Aren't you a jack of all trades?" Hannah said, panting already as she rested her arm.

"I like to try new things. Like you do." He stepped back, surveying their work. Then he pointed. "Missed a spot."

Hannah swatted playfully at him. "Maybe I'll let you finish this part up."

Josh grinned at her and resumed sanding. "You're lucky I like you."

Her heartbeat double-time at the potential she heard in his simple comment. With every stroke of her hand, thoughts of becoming something more with Josh, of sharing his life, echoed in her head. But her smile disappeared when the tornado siren sounded in the distance. Still carrying the sanding block, she ran into the living room to check the news.

"Looks like it's time to take cover," she said when Josh stepped up beside her. "A tornado has been spotted south of Linbeck."

The lights flickered, as if to prove her point, and then went out. In the sudden gloom that enveloped them, Hannah reached for Josh and gripped his arm, feeling panicky. Outside it had grown still and quiet, and she knew that meant a tornado.

"Calm down," he said reassuringly. Josh took her hand and led her into the bathroom. He shut the door and slid down it until he was sitting, elbows resting on his knees. "Nothing to do now but wait it out."

Hannah perched on the toilet, clasping both hands between her knees. "I miss having a basement," she said.

"Yeah, I was thinking the same thing," Josh said from his spot on the floor. "This doesn't feel safe at all."

They listened intently for a minute, but all they could hear was the building creaking.

"We should get in the tub," Hannah whispered. "If you don't have a basement, you get into the tub." A college friend that'd grown up in Texas had given her that bit of information once.

"Yeah, I heard that too, which is why I live in a house with a basement," he retorted. Before she could respond, the wind began howling outside and lightning cracked the sky. It was so near that it shook the walls.

Josh got to his feet. "Ok, let's get in the tub."

Hannah settled into the opposite end of the tub, and he held his arms out to her. In the dim light peeking through the window, she saw that the invitation was sincere and genuine. She scooted around and slid between his legs. Unsure of what to make of their situation, she sat forward to give him space, but Josh gently pulled her back.

"Try to relax," he sighed into her ear.

Instinctively, she hugged his strong arms wrapped around her waist and rested her head on his chest, just below his chin. His heart thumped rhythmically against her back. His steady breaths calmed her, and lit a fire inside as well. Sirens continued to blare and aside from the wind and lightening, it was eerily quiet. Without the usual sound of traffic and beeping horns, Hannah imagined the entire town hiding in their basements and bathtubs.

"I have to be honest," Josh said, his breath caressing her hair. "I don't feel any safer."

She laughed softly. "Me either."

They continued to sit in silence, listening. After a few minutes, a cramping pain began creeping through Hannah's legs. She shifted uncomfortably and felt Josh do the same behind her.

He groaned. "I don't know how much longer I can sit here."

Hannah massaged her legs, trying to shake the heavy feeling. "Me either," she said.

Sitting up awkwardly, Hannah felt her cheek graze his, rough against her skin. The contact made her breath catch, and she hesitated before shifting completely so they were face to face. Josh's breath slid across her lips. In the waning light, she met his eyes. When he didn't break her gaze, Hannah leaned toward him without thinking, her movement so slight that had they been any further apart, it wouldn't have been noticeable. But now their lips touched, just barely, his hot against hers. She could feel his heart beating rapidly against the palm of her hand, and she felt hers match the intensity. Josh closed his eyes as Hannah slid her hand up his chest and into his hair, feeling its silkiness against her fingertips. And as Josh tenderly, fully pressed his lips into hers, the sirens shut off.

The sudden wave of silence served as an interruption, breaking the connection between them. Josh pulled back just as Hannah did, as if physically locked by the electricity between them. For a moment they stared at one another, breathless and confused. Hannah was thankful for the weighty darkness that hid her burning cheeks from Josh's stare.

"Um... I..." Hannah struggled to surface from her temporary disposition. "Sounds like it's all over."

"Yeah..." he mumbled. "Guess I better check it out."

Clumsily, Hannah got to her feet and Josh followed suit, moaning as he shook out his legs. She felt his hand on her arm steadying her as she climbed out of the tub. Then Josh slid around her to open the door but all that greeted them was pitch-blackness.

"Power's still out," she heard him say from somewhere in the dark.

Hannah groped along the wall until she saw the

moonlight streaming in through the living room window, silhouetting Josh's tall, broad body. She stood beside him and resisted the urge to take his hand. Instead, she focused on bright stars, peeking from behind the few remaining clouds, and the glitter of rain on the lawn.

"Looks like the worst is over," he said quietly. Linbeck had survived tornadoes before. No doubt there'd be fallen trees, maybe even downed power lines. And without electricity, they didn't know if another tornado was brewing. She hoped Josh wouldn't leave, would worry if he did, but after what had happened in the tub, she figured dismally he would go. Confused by what was going on between them, Hannah struggled to wrap her mind around their current relationship. Josh still seemed hesitant to get involved with her, and Hannah didn't blame him. Broken trust was something that took time to rebuild. Yet at the same time, she saw him struggling, too, with keeping his distance.

But whether Josh stayed or not, they couldn't continue work on the furniture without light. She had a supply of candles, but not enough to do any quality work. "What now?"

Josh glanced at his wristwatch. "It's almost ten o'clock. Without any power, we may as well go to sleep." He gave her a playful elbow jab. "Somewhere other than the tub."

She felt the butterflies take flight in her stomach at the fact that he was staying. While Hannah fought the urge to tell him there was enough room for the two of them in her bed, she said, "The only option, then, is the floor."

There was a beat of silence. "The floor it is," he said.
Hannah gathered a few blankets and pillows, arranging them on the floor beside her bed.

After settling under the covers, she considered the severity of the situation they'd been in. "I think we should pray," Hannah suggested. She heard the rustle of blankets, and then Josh was beside her on the bed taking her hand.

"Great idea," he said softly.

Hannah began by thanking God for keeping them and their property safe from damage. She also prayed for the people of Linbeck and surrounding towns in the path of the tornado that they, too, were spared. When she finished, Josh squeezed her hand affectionately before returning to his makeshift bed.

While she lay there, Hannah thought of how Josh had come right over almost the instant she'd asked for his help. Silently, she prayed for God to give her insight into her relationship with Josh. She fell asleep with a final request... that whoever she was to be with, loving him would come as easy as it was with Josh.

Somewhere in the middle of the night she felt Josh nudge her over and slide on the bed. He wrapped his arms around her and again, she fell asleep. When the early morning sunlight pierced her dreams, Hannah opened her eyes to see Josh's face inches from hers. He was snoring softly with his arm draped across her chest. Immediately, her heart started thumping.

When his eyes opened, he looked momentarily confused, then smiled sweetly and whispered, "Good morning."

Hannah smiled, hoping she wasn't too much of a mess. But the look in Josh's eyes told her she was anything but, and she felt herself blush.

He stretched and yawned, shielding his eyes from the sun.

"How'd you end up in my bed?" Hannah asked, pinned between him and the edge of the bed.

"Guess I snuck in in my sleep." He laughed softly. "Sorry."

Hannah blushed, suddenly became aware of their bodies touching all the way to their toes. "It's okay," she mumbled.

Josh rolled off the bed and stood, searching for his

watch. Hannah glanced at him out of the corner of her eye, taking in his toned chest and pants that hung low on his hips. His messy hair and sleepy eyes were enough to make her want to pull him back down beside her.

But his hurried state of mind told her he had places to go. Hannah got up and began folding and stacking the blankets from his bed.

"You want breakfast?"

Josh fumbled with his shirt buttons. "Thanks for the offer, but I have a meeting at the church."

"On Saturday?" she asked, watching as he put on his shoes and feeling odd that she was witnessing this side of him. It was as if they'd spent the night together on an intimate level, and while they hadn't, something felt different.

"It's a phone conference with the church in New York. Today was the only time they could arrange."
"I'm sorry. If I'd known you had plans today I wouldn't have asked you to come over last night."

Josh found the mirror in the foyer and began combing his hair with his fingers. "Don't be silly. I wanted to help."

Hannah admitted that he didn't seem the least bit perturbed. Rather, he was quite at home in her little apartment.

"Better get that stain covered before it sits out any longer. And try to wash the brush as best as you can. I'll come by later to help finish the furniture."

Listening to his advice, Hannah allowed herself to acknowledge that something had changed between them. Something subtle, but real nonetheless. She prayed it wasn't a figment of her hopeful imagination.

"Thanks for staying," Hannah said as he shrugged into his jacket.

He opened his mouth to speak, but instead nodded. Hannah waited, sensing he had something to tell her.

Josh took a step closer. On a deep breath, he hesitated, then said, "See you tonight."

Hannah nodded, watching him walk away before closing the door. She did a mental rewind of last night, trying to figure out what happened and when. She'd learned long ago to read Josh like an open book. She knew when he was happy, upset, angry, or playful but she had no idea what he looked like in love.

There were the times at the river that his gaze was so soft and so full, she thought maybe that was it. There were countless weekends at the church helping her dad, and evenings having dinner at Josh's place, trying to eat but laughing too hard to have any kind of appetite when she thought she read love on his face.

Every time their eyes met, Hannah wondered. She wondered if what she felt was there for him, too. If his heart was constantly yearning for her as hers was for him. But she never knew for sure. All she had were the bittersweet days sweeping by in a blur. She knew the touch of his hand, the dimple on his right cheek. She knew his warmth, how safe his arms felt, how her name sounded on his lips, and the depth of his green eyes. It was everything she loved about him.

The harsh reality about her past behavior stung. She must have done something, before she left town, to make him think they were a couple—by leaving, she hurt him deeply. Then she returned, behaving in a cavalier fashion, pregnant, resentful that she was forced to come home. How much more must that have hurt him? Hannah realized Josh needed time, and she had nothing but. So she would go right on loving him... hoping and praying God would show her the way to prove to Josh that she had changed, that he could trust her, that she would never hurt him again.

~ TEN ~

As autumn swept through Linbeck, bringing with it the anticipation of the winter ahead, Hannah dove head-first into her job, determined to do her best. Relieved to be moving forward in her life again, she gladly accepted the challenge. Every article she was assigned, she deliberated over, reviewed and rewrote until it was perfectly polished. She met all the deadlines, volunteered for the stories no one else wanted, and stayed late to do any catch-up work. The satisfaction she got from her job impressed her, making her realize the stagnant lifestyle she'd been living had been getting her nowhere.

Even her social life had taken a turn for the better. Delving out of her comfort zone, Hannah had made it a point to meet a few other girls on the staff and to go out with them on occasion. She thanked God every day for fixing what had seemed an impossibly hopeless situation.

Still, unable to ignore the fact that she had to fight to keep Josh out of her mind throughout the day, or the urgency she felt every evening after work to see him, her love for him was impossible to ignore. Yet Hannah couldn't help wondering if all the wrong moments were testimony that there would never be a right moment. She spent a few days trying to un-love him to no avail.

The leaves turned to brilliant, vibrant colors and then shed their leaves far too soon, turning the landscape bleak with their bare fingers extending to the sky. A few days after Thanksgiving, the sky opened and began feathering out its snowflakes from its warehouse in the heavens. Days passed and still they came, plunging the world in frosty white. The frigid air was numbing and froze the breath. As the snow piled on the ground and steepled against the houses, people were forced to retreat indoors to keep from the biting cold.

Christmas was right around the corner and Linbeck shed its usual façade to celebrate the holidays. Light poles were strung with garland, storefronts were decorated with wreaths and brightly lit Christmas trees, and the annual Ice Festival came alive. Despite the cold, people emerged long enough to window-shop and purchase their Christmas trees from the local tree farms.

With Christmas a week away, Josh invited Hannah to the Ice Festival for a night out. Already December had flown by, everyday full with work and deadlines. Hannah went along, eager for a break.

Wrapped in thick jackets, hats, scarves, and mittens they strolled through the hundreds of glowing ice sculptors, the prisms of light reflecting off the satiny darkness. Big snowflakes drifted down on them, coating everything in velvety white and making the air frigid so that their breath came out in clouds and their cheeks turned rosy. The snow crunched underfoot as they walked, making the transcending quiet seem loud despite the Christmas music that was playing softly over the loudspeakers.

"I can't believe it's the end of the year already," Hannah said, snuggling into herself.

Josh nodded in agreement. "It's gone fast."

"Too fast," Hannah said, stopping in front of an angel carved in the ice. "This was always my favorite."

"No, it wasn't," Josh said, laughing. "It was the reindeer."

Pointing at the glimmering statue in front of her, she corrected him. "No, it was the angel. And I don't care what you say about that one year," she began hastily.

Josh held up two fingers, interrupting her. "Two years. In a row. Both times we had to pry your lips off the reindeer's nose."

Hannah scowled at him. "The second time was a dare, if I recall correctly." They continued their slow walk down the path.

"As if that's a logical explanation," Josh teased, placing a friendly arm around her shoulders.

There was a crackle and a brief moment of silence

over the loudspeaker, and then Frank Sinatra's classic voice floated through the air singing White Christmas.

"Oh," Hannah breathed, turning her head slightly. "This song..."

Josh dropped his arm as they listened to Sinatra's voice drifting over them.

"I remember when I was a little girl, we'd go tree hunting. It was an all day affair and my mom always made a big deal out of it," Hannah recalled, suddenly lost in the memory. "I'd pick out the biggest tree I could find and my poor dad had to drag it back to the car and then into the house. My mom would find our box of decorations and she and I would make cocoa and bake cookies and decorate all day while Dad would sit in his recliner, reading the paper and sneaking cookies."

"When we were all finished decorating and we were stuffed full of cocoa and chocolate, Mom would put Sinatra on and dance, around and around the living room, trying to be funny. And I remember watching my dad watch her. His eyes would light up. He'd laugh and gaze at her with...this look. And I adored how in love they were. Enjoyed seeing how he looked at her. Like she was the most beautiful thing he'd ever seen." Hannah smiled at the memory of it.

Suddenly conscious of Josh watching her, she turned her gaze to the glittering ice castle in front of them. "I've always wanted a man to look at me like that. To be able to show me how much he loved me just by the look in his eyes," she said quietly.

Josh watched her as she spoke. When she finished, he held his hand out to her.

She glanced questioningly at it. "What?"

He grinned. "Lets dance."

"Here? There's people watching...no way..." Hannah looked around, her cheeks already flushing.

Josh grabbed her hand and pulled her to him. "Who cares what anyone thinks? There won't ever be another moment like this."

Hannah glanced around again then looked up at him, into those deep green eyes that melted her heart. "Okay," she said, unsure.

They started dancing, awkward in their heavy jackets. People stared and whispered as they passed, but all Hannah could hear was Frank's mellow words echoing through the loudspeaker and falling around them with the snow.

"Want to know the most beautiful thing I've ever seen?" Josh asked, staring intently into her eyes.

She nodded with a smile.

"It was the year our families went to New York for Christmas vacation, right before your mom left," he began. "We were all ice skating in Central Park and you and I were racing around, going as fast as we could. There was this second when I looked over at you and it was as if everything went into slow motion. The city lights were behind you, the snow was falling into your hair, your pink scarf was blowing behind you, and you were laughing. You looked so happy and carefree in that one second, and it was the most beautiful I'd ever seen you," he paused, his eyes soft. "It was the first time I knew I loved you."

Hannah stopped dancing, unsure of what she'd heard. Then without hesitation, Josh leaned down and kissed her. His lips were warm, moist and insistent. She was stunned, caught off guard, and before she could react he pulled back to look at her. Their eyes locked and the silence stretched between them while Josh's words seemed to hang in the air.

"You love me?" she finally whispered.

He raised his hand to her face, slowly and gently cupping her cheek in his palm. His fingers brushed her lips, then traced down her neck and over the sensitive soft skin below her ear. She closed her eyes under his touch, reveling in the trail of heat left by his fingers.

"Always." He brought his lips to hers again, softly at first, then deeper and hungrier. He stole her breath away, surrounded her in a deep, tender passion that engulfed her in a sea of sweet kisses. She kissed him back, hungry and anxious for more, not wanting to stop. All the years they'd been apart flooded through her, making her cling to him and love him even more.

They finally pulled apart, their breathing shaky as they leaned against one another. Hannah looked into his eyes while she tried to calm her heart.

"You remembered that I was wearing a pink scarf?"

Josh laughed. "I remember everything about that moment, just like I'll remember everything about this one," he said, pressing another kiss against her lips.

"What took you so long?" She murmured.

He breathed in deeply and fingered a strand of her hair. "I didn't want to be your second mistake."

Hannah stared at him unable to believe he could ever think such a thing. "Ben was my second mistake," she corrected him. "Not being with you was my first."

Josh stared at her, looking slightly surprised, doubtful. Then his face softened as a smile slowly spread across his face. He wrapped his arms tightly around her. Hannah glanced over Josh's shoulder, suddenly realizing they had an audience of staring people.

"We should keep walking." Feeling her cheeks on fire, she giggled.

Josh grabbed her hand and they continued down the rows of sculptors. Hannah looked at him. "I love you too, you know," she said shyly, leaning into him.

He smiled tenderly at her and put his arm around her shoulders. "I know."

And in his gaze, she saw it. The look that had probably been there all along, but she'd been too blind to see. It said the same thing her father's eyes had said all those years ago. It was the gaze of a man truly, deeply in love.

~ ELEVEN ~

Walking into her dark apartment, Hannah shed her heels and stretched her tired toes. Turning on the light, she deposited her purse and keys on the table and then flipped through the stack of mail she'd been neglecting.

Overwhelmed, she gave up and tossed them aside. She went to the refrigerator where she stared at the bare shelves and contemplated briefly on what she should eat. The choice was between a browning salad, a jar of pickles, and an apple. Sighing, she grabbed the apple and leaned against the kitchen counter, staring at the silence while her thoughts drifted to Josh. She smiled and her heart fluttered as she replayed their kiss. It had been the only thing on her mind the past week, and every time her thoughts got to the end of that night, they rewound back to the beginning.

Just then, the ring of the phone penetrated her thoughts.

"Hello," she sang, already knowing who it was.

"Hey hon," her father said. "I'm going to swing by and drop off some food."

"Food? Since when do you cook?" Hannah asked, munching on the apple.

He laughed. "I don't that often. One of the ladies at church made me a casserole. It's too much for me and I know your eating habits, so I figured you could use it more than I could."

Hannah opened her mouth in mock offense. "I have great eating habits, what are you talking about?"

"What did you eat for dinner?" She glanced at the apple in her hand and thought about the contents in her fridge.

"That's what I thought." He chuckled at her silence. "I'll be there in a few minutes."

Hanging up the phone, Hannah felt relieved dinner was on the way. While she could cook, and did so most nights of the week, today was one of those days she wasn't

in the mood to rummage through her recipe books or de-
frost anything.

True to his word, five minutes later her father let
himself in. "I come bearing gifts," he bellowed.

"Ooh," Hannah said, rushing to him to take the still-
warm pan from his hands. "My mouth is watering already."
Breathing in its tasty aroma deeply, the smell of garlic and
roasted onion made her stomach growl.

"Mine has been the entire ride over." He followed
her into the tiny kitchen.

"So who made it?" she asked, peeling the foil back
and sneaking a peek.

"You don't know her," her dad answered quickly.

Hannah eyed him suspiciously as she grabbed two
plates from the cupboard. "I probably do. I've been going
to church every Sunday for six months and I know most everyone in the congregation."

Her dad busied himself by tidying up her already
spotless kitchen. "Michelle Klausen," he mumbled.

Her mouth fell open. "Dad! You two are seeing each
other, aren't you?"

Everyone in the church knew Michelle not only because she was a faithful attendee, but also because she
was the owner of the local flower shop. After her husband
died ten years earlier in a tragic car accident, leaving
Michelle alone with two children, she'd struggled to keep
their business afloat. Yet she'd managed, and gave her
children the best life she could with an absent father and
husband.

Hannah's dad avoided her accusing stare but the
fierce blush in his cheeks gave him away.

"How long?" she asked, smiling. In hindsight, she recalled how often he'd claimed to be busy when she would
call and the silly grin that was always on his face in recent
weeks.

Despite his happiness, though, Michael looked
ashamed while he confessed. "A few months. I couldn't tell

you, Hannah. I didn't want you to feel betrayed."

"Betrayed?" Hannah felt her heart ache at the fact that he would ever even think that. "I'm happy for you, Dad. You could never betray me. Mom's the one that did that, not you." She gave him a big hug, trying to reassure him that she meant it.

He looked relieved. "I've been worried about it from the beginning."

"I'm twenty-three. You don't have to worry about me anymore," she said, patting him on the arm.

He pushed his glasses up on the bridge of his nose. "You're only twenty-three. I'll always worry."

"I know, but not about things like that. I'm glad you've found someone to make you happy again." Hannah said affectionately, patting him on the arm. "Are you sure you don't want to stay for dinner? I can't eat all this by myself."

Michael grabbed a fork from the drawer and took a quick bite straight from the pan. "Mmm," he moaned.

"Tempting. But I have to run to the church and get things ready for the Wednesday night service." He rinsed the fork off and slid it into the dishwasher.

Disappointed at his early departure, Hannah walked him to the door. "Maybe I'll come by in a while to help out."

Shaking his head, he pulled her into a gentle hug. "You need to get some rest. Between work, church, and Josh, you haven't given yourself any time to relax."

She leaned into him, feeling the first traces of wariness sinking behind her eyelids. "I think I will retire early tonight. Thanks for dinner."

"No problem, Hon." He reached for the doorknob then stopped short. "Oh, hey, I almost forgot to tell you. I'm having a going away party for Josh this Sunday afternoon. It's short notice, but I thought you'd want to help."

Hannah looked blankly at him. "Going away? Where's he going?"

Her dad blinked. He stared at her for a minute then turned back to the door and swung it open.

"Nowhere. My mistake," he mumbled, hurriedly.

Hannah grabbed his arm, stopping him. Her heart was suddenly beating fast. "Dad, where is Josh going?"

He sighed miserably, now at a loss for words. "Honey, I think you need to talk to Josh about it. It's not my place."

Her mind rushed in a tumble of thoughts. She didn't know what was going on, or why Josh would even consider leaving. He'd told her he loved her. The tears were already welling up in her eyes.

"Dad," Hannah pleaded. "Tell me, please?"

Her dad's face looked pained, but he stepped back into her apartment and shut the door softly behind him. "The church in New York needs him. It's been an ongoing thing for the past six months or more, and they recently got serious about it. He agreed to go a couple of days ago. That's all I can tell you."

Hannah sat on her couch in stunned silence while she listened. She suddenly remembered that first Sunday she'd gone to her dad's church and Erin had mentioned the New York thing. And the morning after the tornado when he had a phone meeting with them. Now it was the end of the year, just as Josh said it would be when they would know more.

She felt a roller coaster of emotions at war inside her. As her dad's words sank in, an overwhelming anger had pulsed its way into her stomach, throat, and head. It snaked through her veins, making her blood boil. She got to her feet, her cheeks on fire. Why didn't Josh talk to her about it before accepting the offer? Why did it seem everyone else knew and she didn't?

Swallowing her tears, she angrily snatched her purse and keys from the table, completely forgetting to grab her jacket until they stepped out into the frigid air.

"Hannah, are you all right?" her father asked, his

worry apparent when she returned with her coat.

She controlled her breathing and forced the words, each one coming out in white puffs as they collided with the cold. "I'm fine. I'm going to go talk to him, is all."

He eyed her with skepticism. Finally he nodded and followed her to their cars, casting worried sideways glances at her.

"We've been waiting on them for a while now, and then one day they called…"

Hannah didn't even hear her dad trying to make her feel better. All she could focus on was the leaden feeling in the pit of her stomach, as if someone had slugged her. She didn't know whether to be angry, hurt, sad, or all of them at once. While she felt betrayed, Hannah still felt a glimmer of hope that her father had it all wrong. Josh would explain it to her, and this would all go away. After all, they'd just confessed their love to one another after a lifetime of friendship, Hannah reasoned. She'd proven to him that she had changed, and now she would promise to keep changing if it meant he would stay.

The thought of losing Josh made her want to weep, made her heart ache with thoughts of what could be. They were only beginning - they couldn't be over yet.

Hannah climbed into her car, mumbling something to her dad before cranking the engine to life. Her hands felt numb as if someone else were inside her skin doing all the things she should be doing, but her mind was far away.

Her thoughts went over the past, suddenly recalling all the times Josh had looked at her the way he had the night at the Ice Festival. He'd loved her for so long, she thought, furious at herself for not seeing it years ago. As she drove, her anger slowly subsided. Soon she found herself in a pool of tears, sobbing and mopping her face with a napkin she'd found in the glove box. It was hard to see the white, snow blown roads around her tears and her car was slipping and sliding as she drove. Finally she slowed down, ignoring the irritated honks behind her as she hunched over the steering wheel and squinted miserably out the wind-shield.

By the time she pulled into Josh's drive, Hannah managed to pull herself somewhat together. Taking a deep breath, she got out of the car and carefully made her way over the slick drive to his front door. She knocked, waiting and trying to hold on to the last shred of hope that had re-kindled itself in her heart. Until Josh confirmed what her dad said, there was still a chance.

A muffled "come in" sounded from inside and Han-nah walked through the door, half expecting to see packing boxes and tape.

"I'll be out in a minute!" Josh hollered from one of the bedrooms.

She waited numbly in front of the living room win-dows, gazing into her once again uncertain future. Sudden-ly she felt Josh's arms slip around her waist and he tender-ly nuzzled her neck.

"Hey, Baby. I missed you." She could hear the smile in his voice.

Still suppressing tears, Hannah stiffened under his touch. She didn't want to look at him, didn't want to hear him say what she feared.

"What's wrong?" Josh asked, alarm sounding in his voice as he turned her toward him.

Hannah swallowed and looked up at him. She was so glad he couldn't see what was going on inside her. Her heart fluttered and turned, her breathing felt labored, her stomach twisted, and her palms sweated. But the second he saw her face, she knew he could read her like a book.

"Your dad told you," he said, his voice low.

"So it's true?" Hannah heard the quiet desperation dripping from her words. "You're going?"

Josh dropped his eyes from hers, his expression un-readable as he nodded. Hannah stepped away from him, her pain stinging.

"I didn't want you to find out like this," he said. "I

found out the other day and I've been trying to figure out how to tell you…" His words lingered in the air between them as he watched her.

"What about your house?" Realizing this was really happening, Hannah felt like her world was breaking in pieces.

Josh exhaled. "I already talked with a realtor. It's going up this weekend. My parents have a Power of Attorney to take care of things while I'm away."

Unable to match his stare anymore, Hannah looked at her feet. She didn't want to ask the question, knowing how selfish it would sound, but it was inevitable. She had to know. "What about me?"

Josh reached for her, but Hannah stepped away from him without even thinking. When she saw his face, she wished she hadn't. She was so vulnerable right now, though; she felt that any touch would set her off in a heap of tears.

"Sit down, Hannah. Please," he pleaded. "We need to talk about this."

Hesitantly, she gave in and sat next to him on the couch. Josh scooted closer, forcing their knees to touch.

Trying to hide the waver in her voice, Hannah began before Josh could. "What's going to happen with us?" The fear and hurt were evident in her voice, but she was beginning to see how hopeless the situation was. Hannah had a chance to have Josh and love him, but she'd waited too long. Now their lives were different, clashing at the worst possible moment. "You're going to New York," she reminded him. "What did you think was going to happen to us?"

Josh cleared his throat uncomfortably and looked at the ground. "I'm not going to New York."

Confused, Hannah stared at him. "What? My dad said… you said…"

"I'm going to Nigeria," he said flatly.

Hannah blinked, her entire body trembling. "Nigeria? You… I—" she stammered in disbelief.

142

He grabbed her hand. "Listen, okay? Let me explain."

The tears came again, flooding her eyes and making rivers down her cheeks. Hannah swiped unsuccessfully at them, but they kept coming. Pulling her hand from his, she slid away, suddenly not wanting his consolation. Nothing he said, short of 'I'm not going' would ease her pain.

"When do you leave?" she managed, her voice wavering.

"I go to New York on Monday to go over specifics. I'll be back after that for a few days, then I go to Nigeria." Swallowing a sob, Hannah felt herself crumbling. "For how long?"

Unable to look at her, Josh stared at his hands. "I don't know. It could be a couple months, it could be a year."

Numbly, Hannah got to her feet, wanting to make a getaway. It was too much at once. Only thirty minutes earlier she'd been at home, anticipating a delicious dinner and daydreaming about Josh. Now, her whole world was upside down. She needed to think, grasp things in her mind. Losing Josh had never been a question in the past. He'd always been there and she dumbly assumed he always would. And now, he wouldn't be in Linbeck loving her. Now he'd be across the world without her.

"Let me talk, Baby. Let me explain," Josh said, seeing her step toward the door.

Hannah stared longingly at it, wanting to get away from here, his arms, his eyes, and everything about him that hurt so much. Instead, she hesitantly reclaimed her seat beside him on the couch.

Looking relieved, Josh explained, "The family that's in Nigeria now has been there for two years. About a year ago, they built a church and a school in the village, which was doing great. They were really reaching the villagers. But six months ago, their little girl started getting sick and for the past few months, she's been up and down with a virus none of the doctors over there can treat. Now she's taken a turn for the worse and they've decided they need to go back to New York to get some professional medical help. Someone needs to be there to keep the church and the school running. Someone needs to keep helping those people." His voice sounded urgent, as if it were imperative that she understand.

Which she did. As much as Hannah didn't want to, she completely understood. After hanging around him the past six months, she'd seen his passion for helping, for reaching out to the hurting. It was a part of who he was, and it was a part of him she'd fallen in love with. The right thing to do, she knew, was to let him go without giving him a hard time so he could focus on the mission, not her. Yet it still hurt her, still too fresh to blow him a kiss and send him across the world. She loved him and was so sure that he was the one.

"I've been on a lot of missions already, I'm a youth pastor. They need me," Josh explained.

"So, I guess that means, what? We're through?" As soon as she said it, she broke down sobbing.

Josh gently took her hand and slowly pulled her to him. Wiping the wet streams from her cheeks, he tipped her face up so she was looking at him through a blurry wall of tears. "I know everything is happening fast. And I know it's hard for you to understand where I'm coming from—"

"No, no," Hannah interrupted. "I understand. I really do. I just... Josh, I can't do the long distance thing. I've tried before and it doesn't work."

He suddenly stood, looking nervous. "I don't want to do that, either."

Fumbling clumsily with his pocket, he withdrew a small, silver ring with a diamond perched on top. Hannah stared at it in disbelief as he sat beside her, the ring pinched between his fingers. "I had a big, elaborate evening planned," Josh said, still holding it awkwardly in front of her. "But things haven't gone exactly the way I wanted." He laughed a little, but his smile dimmed as if he realized the situation was too serious to be taken lightly.

"I've spent a lifetime loving you, Hannah, and I was hoping I could spend the rest of it with you." He paused as if expecting an immediate answer. When she didn't say anything, he reached down and grabbed her hand.

Tenderly, he slid the ring on her finger and they both stared at it in silence. "Will you marry me?"

The ring was so beautiful it took Hannah's breath away and made her feel dizzy. This was the moment she'd been waiting for as long as she could remember. As a little girl, she'd always dreamed of who her groom would be and now it was the one man she'd never have thought it to be. But marrying him wouldn't mean a little house and babies and soccer practice. It would mean moving to Nigeria.

Seconds passed, but Hannah couldn't respond. His expectancy turned into a frown as he watched her. The words wouldn't come though she willed them to. She could hear them in her mind but her mouth wasn't cooperating.

Finally, she looked up at him. "I can't, Josh," she said in a near whisper, almost choking on her words.

His hurt and disappointment were evident, but he nodded. "Well," he said, slowly dropping his hand to his side. "I was hoping you wouldn't say that, but I guess I expected it."

Trembling, Hannah began sliding the ring off her finger, but Josh stopped her. "Keep it," he said sadly. "I'll marry you someday." He tried to smile but failed and he turned away from her.

She stared at his back, fighting the urge to wrap her arms around him and kiss it all away. Instead, she made her way to the door and opened it, knowing the second it shut behind her, her life would never be the same again. She ignored her mind begging her to turn around, ignored the longing in her broken heart, and ignored the pain written all over Josh's face as he turned to watch her leave. And doing what she was best at, Hannah walked away.

~ * ~

"Hannah," her dad called out. "Open the door, I need to talk to you."

Hannah shuffled to the door and cracked it open. When her dad walked in, he shut it behind him and stared compassionately at his distraught daughter. Hannah knew she looked like a train wreck. She could feel her swollen, puffy eyes from crying and her nose was running, so she sniffled and dabbed at it with a crumpled up Kleenex.

"Oh sweetie," Michael said, hugging Hannah.

Hannah sobbed and clung to him. Josh had taken what was left of her heart. After she'd left his place two days earlier, the reality of her future filled the emptiness in her chest with the bitter truth. There would never be another man that could live up to what Josh was to her.

Apart of her knew she was stupid for not taking a chance with him, but the other part was scared of marriage under these circumstances, of losing her best friend for good, but mainly she was terrified of Nigeria. She'd heard awful things about places like that. Aside from the poverty, there were plenty of things to fear. Like the horrendous treatment of women in certain areas, diseases, scary bugs and animals, intense heat. How could she willingly walk in-to that kind of environment? How could Josh keep her safe from the realities of a cold, mean world?

She'd prayed, gone over it in her mind, but she was too scared. Hannah wasn't missionary material and if Josh discovered that while they were over there, she was afraid he would think he made a mistake by marrying her. And when she let her mind take over, she realized that Josh was facing all the same dangers she would be, if not more. What if he didn't come home? What if something happened to him and he had thought she didn't love him as much as she did?

Hannah had even gone as far as writing a comparison list of pros and cons of going or staying, but in the end the sides were equal. She couldn't compare her love for Josh to living in a grass hut, so she ended up tearing it to pieces and tossing it in the trash. Despite the pain, she remained rooted to her decision and waited for a sign from God to tell her different. After all, she'd reasoned, time would heal. Time had healed the wounds from Ben and losing her baby, but Hannah knew full well that Josh had helped that process.

After a long while of sobbing into her father's once starched shirt, Hannah finally sat up, wiping her nose and hiccupping. "He's... he's really going, Dad. I don't know what to do. He asked me to marry him and I told him no," she began crying again.

Her dad frowned deeply and led her to the couch. "Josh told me everything. Honey, he's worried to death about you. So am I," he said sincerely, forcing her to look at him. "It's been two days and you haven't answered your phone or your door."

He was right. Josh had tried everything to talk to her. He called relentlessly, left message after message, went to her apartment and knocked until she thought he'd wear a hole in her door. A co-worker even told her he'd shown up looking for her at the office. Still Hannah couldn't bring herself to talk to him or take his calls. She missed him so much, but when she thought of him leaving and the deep wound it stirred deep down, her sadness would reawaken until it left her weak with sorrow. Her courage had long since abandoned her. It seemed all she could do was hole herself up in her room, watching the days come and go, bringing her closer to the morning when Josh would leave.

"I don't know if I did the right thing. I love him, I really do, but Nigeria? What about my job, my apartment, you? What if we get there and I realize I made a huge mistake? Or worse, Josh realizes he made a mistake marrying me," she cried.

Her dad put his arm around Hannah's shoulders. "First of all, don't worry about me. I've been fine all these years on my own and although I missed you like crazy, I'm still here. Second of all, jobs and apartments are a dime a dozen, sweetie. They come and go and there will always be another one."

Hannah gazed at him through her tears. "You think I should go, don't you?"

Michael shook his head. "I didn't say that. But I don't want you to make any decision worrying about everything and everyone else. You said you love him. And I know the man loves you. Honestly, if there is any guy in the world I'd want to have my daughter, it'd be Josh."

Hannah wiped her nose and dropped her hands in her lap, tugging on the Kleenex. "I can't do it, Dad. I've thought about it and thought about it and I...can't."

Her dad looked at her over his glasses. "You can do it, but you aren't putting your faith in the right place. You're relying on yourself, on Josh. You need to be relying on God." His words stung.

"I've prayed. Over and over again," Hannah responded, somewhat defensively. "I know I love him, know Josh is the one, but...I'm not a missionary. I'm just someone who's still putting herself back together, who's picking up the pieces from a series of bad decisions. I'm not like Josh who's helped so many people find their way—including me..."

"Hannah," Michael began. He pinned Hannah down with a sincere look over his glasses. "You've done such a beautiful job of transforming yourself and your life. You need to stop trying so hard and take a long, hard look at what God's already done in you. He's made you strong, made you an overcomer. You are fully equipped to go with Josh and change a part of the world. God's blessed you with the love of a man that will guide you and help you. He's given you a solid foundation here at home with a congregation that will support and pray for you both. And you've already helped dozens of people. Not in the way Josh does, but in your own way - in the way God created you to.

"Those kids in the youth group adore you, they look up to you. The folks at the homeless shelter look forward to seeing you. The women at the church have told me how blessed they've been since you've come home. So whether you realize it or not, you can and have helped people. You are ready to go to Nigeria. You're only challenge is to get past the hurdle you've put in the way. Yourself."

He let his words sink in for a moment before going to the kitchen where he began pulling ingredients from the cupboards and fridge, leaving Hannah stunned at the truth her father had just spoke.

"I'm making you dinner. And then you're going to shower, pack a bag, and come home with me. And tomorrow, you're going to church to say goodbye to Josh."

It'd been years since her dad used that tone with her, but even now it snapped her out of the daze she'd been in for days. Obediently, she did as she was told, dreading Sunday with all her heart.

~ TWELVE ~

To everyone else it was just another Sunday, only with free food after the service. To Hannah, it was a day closer to what felt like the end of her world. People bustled around her, talking and laughing and carrying on. The air carried the aroma of hot food and baked desserts and with it came a festive atmosphere.

Yet while the rest of the world kept going, Hannah sat in the back row, sadly watching Josh on stage talk and laugh with the rest of the choir, feeling as though time for her had stopped. Tomorrow he would leave and she would be in Linbeck for the first time in her life without him.

"Go talk to him." Her dad had slipped into the seat beside her unnoticed.

Hannah managed a weak smile. "I will. Later."

So far Josh didn't even know she was there. Trying to buy a little more time before saying goodbye, Hannah had quietly taken a seat near the back so she could collect her thoughts. Although she'd spent the night thinking about what her father had said, she had still fretted and fussed, tossed and turned, finally making her mind up about one thing. Trying the long distance relationship. It would be hard, if not impossible seeing how Josh wouldn't have easy accessibility to a phone or computer, but she would do it for him. Breaking up wasn't the answer, going with him was still too terrifying, so that left one alternative: a traditional relationship by letters and the occasional phone call. Maybe even a surprise homecoming, she'd imagined the night before. Where Josh would appear on her doorstep with nothing but his backpack and his heart on his sleeve, telling her he couldn't live without her.

"You never were good with dealing with your problems," Michael was saying, interrupting her daydream as he rested his hand sympathetically on her knee. "Even as a little girl, you holed your feelings up and could never talk about them. I think that's the one thing you got from your mom."

Hannah sighed and placed her hand over her father's. "I'm fine, Dad. I am. I don't know if I can say goodbye to him."

"I know it's hard, Hannah. Sometimes decisions like these don't always have a clear answer. And sometimes you need to step out in faith. Either way, I'm sure you'll make the right decision."

Hannah nodded with a pat on his hand. "Thanks."

Michael got up, squeezing her shoulder as he headed up front as people began taking their seats for worship.

Hannah's mind drifted the entire service. Her thoughts tumbled over the past couple weeks, from the Ice Festival to the preceding days, trying to think back to any sign there may have been that Josh had been keeping a secret from her. There hadn't been any, though. He'd been completely normal, except in love. Maybe that was where she'd missed it. In the past she'd always turned a blind eye to Josh's affection for her, leaving her on unfamiliar territory with him. She'd only known him as a friend, never on such an intimate level.

Hannah suddenly realized that when he'd found out he was leaving, he'd probably planned to propose. So instead of worrying about their separation, he'd worried about her answer.

She sighed, feeling her head throb from the constant bombardment of questions and thoughts. It seemed ages ago when everything was perfect. Only two weeks earlier she was entertaining the idea of spending a lifetime with Josh. Now how long would she have to wait? A month? Six months? A year? They'd both already spent so long searching for the right person and when they thought they'd found them...

The hour passed too quickly. Hannah dreaded having to say goodbye—was never good at them. Instead, she wanted to go home, curl up in a cave of blankets, and sleep through tomorrow. But as she got to her feet, she saw Josh scanning the dispersing crowd, undoubtedly looking for her. Hannah felt the wall she'd been trying to put up dissolve as she approached him. He was silent, but his eyes showed his relief that she was there. Josh reached down and grabbed her hand, his fingers brushing the ring still on her finger.

"You're still wearing it," he said quietly as he gently caressed her hand.

She shivered under the familiarity of his touch. "I never took it off."

They stared uncertainly at one another.

"I miss you," Hannah blurted, feeling the tears brimming in her eyes. "Don't go. Please."

Josh brushed aside a strand of hair that had fallen in her eyes. "I have to. I'm sorry."

Hannah took a deep breath and quickly wiped the tears away. "You leave today?"

Nodding, he kept his gaze fixed on her. "This afternoon. But I'll be back in two weeks before I go to Nigeria."

Searching his handsome face, she realized he was giving her more time to think about his proposal. The tears returned as she imagined the empty days ahead.

"I have to say goodbye right now, or I'll..." she choked on the last of her words and wiped her eyes with a shaky hand.

Josh cupped her cheek, and then slid his hand into her hair as he pulled her face to his. Gently but desperately, he kissed her for only a second before enveloping her in his arms. Hannah clung to him, trying to remember every detail of how he felt against her so she would have at least a part of him while he was gone.

"My offer still stands, Hannah," he said into her ear. "I'll wait as long as it takes."

She pulled away from him and managed a weak smile. "I'll be here when you get back," she said, turning her attention to his collar so she wouldn't start crying again. Straightening it with her fingers, Hannah added, "and then you can ask me again."

Josh sighed deeply, his green eyes looking pained. "Until then, if you change your mind-"

"I'll know where to find you." Summoning all her willpower, she turned to go, then stopped and looked at him over her shoulder. "Be careful."

"Hey," he said quickly, catching her hand. He leaned down close to her ear and whispered, "I love you, Baby."

Those four words made Hannah almost change her mind. She almost threw her fear and rationale out the door, just to keep him close to her, just to be able to be near him and touch and love him forever. Then the overpowering sense of panic returned. Hugging him a final time, she told him, "I love you, too."

Josh watched her go, looking distressed. As Hannah reached her car, she turned one last time to wave goodbye. Their eyes met and in that fleeting moment their pain and longing crossed. Then it was caught in the wind and distance between them, lying dormant and waiting for the next encounter. Hannah didn't know when that would be.

~ * ~

She woke up the next day to a blinding ray of sunlight that had worked its way through the curtains. Trying to stay in the rich darkness of her sleep, Hannah pulled the covers tighter around her head, but it was too strong to block out. She pushed the blankets aside and cracked an eye open, squinting. Today was just another day without Josh, and suddenly the sun didn't seem so bright.

Returning to work for the first time in a week didn't seem as rewarding or challenging. A few of the girls in her office invited her out to dinner later in the evening, but it didn't sound appealing. She went anyway and the once lively conversations that drew her in seemed boring, and the once excellent food was tasteless. Instead, Hannah retreated to her dad's so often she wondered why she was still paying rent at her apartment.

"I'm here," Hannah called down the hallway one evening after work.

Pots clanged. "In the kitchen."

Tossing her purse and keys on the table in the entry, she shed her coat and followed the smell of baked salmon.

"Smells good," she told him with a quick kiss on his cheek. "Need any help?"

"Sure. You stir these vegetables while I get the fish on the table," Michael said, passing her the wooden spoon. "How was work?"

"Actually, pretty good. I was assigned to cover the Allen County bank robber story," she told him, feeling proud. "If I do well with this it could lead to bigger, better stories, maybe even a promotion."

"That's great," Michael exclaimed, setting the sizzling entrée on a hot pad in the middle of the table. "And how are those girls you've been hanging out with? What're their names again? Olivia and..."

"Shawna. They're fine. A little piqued that I got the story, but happy for me nonetheless," Hannah said with a grin.

"They should be. You've worked hard enough for it."

Hannah turned the stove off and transferred the pot to the sink to drain the vegetables. "Oh, I almost forgot. Olivia was asking me about baptisms. They don't have a church and her six year old son has suddenly taken an interest in getting baptized."

She dumped the veggies in a bowl and set them next to the salmon. While Michael whipped up some potatoes, Hannah gathered the plates and silverware and set the table.

"Of course. I'd never turn down a child. Give her my number and tell her to call me." His face suddenly lit up. "Speaking of calling someone, Josh called today."

Hannah knew that Josh called him every day. Her dad managed to slip it in to every conversation they had. Josh had called her too, as he had every day since he left. Their conversations were always the same: how his day was, how hers was, how much they missed each other,

Hannah crying.

Still, Hannah felt her insides immediately start rolling at the mention of his name. "What'd he have to say today?" she asked, trying to sound nonchalant as she took a seat and waited for her dad.

"Just more briefings and meetings. He's slowly getting filled in on the nitty-gritty details. And of course, he asked about you."

Hannah perked up. "What'd you tell him?"

"The usual. You're still moping around, coming by every night after work, telling me how much you miss him and that I think you're reconsidering his offer." He stole a glance at her.

"Did you really tell him that?" Hannah asked, sitting up quickly.

Michael brought the potatoes to the table and sat next to her. "In so many words." He gazed at her over his glasses. "Hannah, honey, you do realize your last chance is a week away? After his short visit here to wrap up the loose ends, he's gone. For a long time."

She nodded. "I know. It's all I think about."

Michael grinned at her, sensing enough to lighten the mood. "Have you come up with anything yet?"

Hannah smiled back. "You'll be the first to know when I have, Dad."

He nodded, accepting her answer, and got up to get the pitcher of tea they'd forgotten on the counter. "Almost forgot," Michael muttered, squeezing Hannah's shoulder as he passed. "So," he set the jug on the table and slid back into his seat. "How 'bout them Bears?"

Hannah laughed with a shake of her head. "Not doing so well," she said, going along with the change of subject.

They prayed over their food and spent the rest of the meal talking about everyday matters, like the cost of gas and how much Hannah spent a week driving back and forth to his house.

She convinced her dad to relax in the living room while she cleaned up. Hannah realized it went like this every night. She showed up after work, her dad asked her a seemingly innocent question that inevitably led to Josh, a small lecture or word of encouragement, and the welcomed change of subject. Realizing it was her father's way of stressing that time was getting shorter, Hannah went along with it.

After the kitchen was spotless, she gathered her things and went to say goodbye. "I'll talk to you tomorrow." She gave him a hug and light kiss on the cheek.

"Tell Josh I said hi when you talk to him," he said with a wink.

While driving home, she thought about what her father had said. Time was short. Josh would be back to Linbeck in a week for a couple days, and then he would fly off to another continent, another world. At least now he was only a few states away, but that fact brought little comfort. Soon enough he would be gone.

~ * ~

A couple mornings later, Hannah woke up, dreading the long week ahead of her. She tried to think of something to cheer her up, excite her, make her smile, but the only thing that did was the thought of Josh coming home, even if it was only for a few days. In the early morning light, Hannah held up her hand, watching the prisms of sunlight reflect off the diamond. She remembered the look in his eyes when he'd asked her to marry him and how tender and loving they were. She recalled how his fingers shook as he'd slid the ring on, so nervous, but gentle. She thought of his love that she'd had for so long without even realizing it. All these things welled up within her, created an urgency to see him and be with him, no matter what the cost.

She could barely make it through two weeks without him, let alone some unknown amount of time with hardly any contact. She loved him, more than she'd ever loved before. Even her fear of the unknown, Hannah finally concluded, wasn't enough to keep her from what she knew in her heart to be right.

Hannah got up and began getting ready for work, her mind suddenly made up and her stomach twisting in anticipation. She didn't want to think of what she was doing, she was going to do it and there was only one week to get everything in order.

~ * ~

Josh's eyes were as green as they ever had been. His hair was a little longer and unruly, but his goatee was neatly trimmed. Dressed in nothing more than jeans and an old t-shirt with a backpack slung over his shoulder, he looked so painfully handsome it took her breath away.

Hannah took a deep breath, suddenly so nervous she was tingling all over. When they'd spoken that morning, she hadn't let him know that she would be there, waiting for him.

The past week had been long and crazy and had exhausted her, but sleep had not come the night before. She was out of a job, out of an apartment, and right back where she'd started six months earlier—in her old room at her dad's house. Her passport had been expedited, her papers in order.

A still-shocked, but understanding, Olivia and Shawna had rushed her to the nearest bridal shop as soon as Hannah explained her situation. Erin and a few other women from church, after hearing what was going on from Michael, organized a cooking party to cater the wedding and Michelle Klausen donated her entire supply of white irises. While Hannah was getting her dress fitted, her papers filed, passports ordered, and rings financed, her friends, family, and even Josh's parents decorated her dad's church.

The morning of Josh's arrival, Hannah had swung by the church before going to the airport. Feeling frazzled and tired, she'd only hoped for a few vases of flowers and some candles. After all, what could she expect for a wedding slapped together in a matter of days? But standing in the wide archway leading to the darkened sanctuary, she'd felt herself choke up, felt the grateful tears well in her eyes as they took in the transformation. Even in the shadows, the church had gone from a simple, conventional look to a romantic chapel that took Hannah's breath away. Gorgeous white irises were everywhere. At the end of each row of pews, sprouting magnificently out of vases that surrounded the stage, on the tables and the altar, even dotting the floor in various places. Candles were mixed in with the flowers and Hannah knew their mellow glow would create a dreamy atmosphere.

"Hey sweetie," her dad had said quietly while he stood beside her, his hands in his pockets.

"This... this is..." Her words seemed to be locked in her throat.

Michael had nodded. A small, satisfied smile rested on his face. "It is, isn't it?"

"Dad," Hannah had whispered, turning and giving him a squeezing hug. "Thank you so much."

He'd hugged her back. "I'm so proud of you, Hannah," he'd said into her hair. "You've become a remarkable young woman. Josh is a lucky man."

Hannah had pulled back, overwhelmed at the emotions churning inside her. Fear, excitement, longing, nervousness, love. "Let's hope he meant what he said about keeping the offer on the table." She'd laughed, hearing it echo off the tall sanctuary walls.

"You better go get him, then. What are you waiting for?"

Now here she was at the airport, heart hammering in her chest, and discovering how nerve racking it was to propose to someone you couldn't live without.

She walked toward him through the swarm of people, seemingly unnoticed. When he stood next to baggage claim, he looked up and saw her. Immediately his face softened, despite his obvious surprise. Hannah walked up to him, smiling. Josh dropped his bag to the floor in a heap and pulled her to him in one fluid motion. His scent and cologne filled her senses and she was lost in his familiar arms that held her close as if he didn't want to let her go.

"I can't believe how much I've missed you," he said softly in her ear.

It took her a moment to find the words. "Me too. I've been miserable without you," she confessed.

Josh pulled away to look at her. His eyes met hers and there was so much that passed between them in that couple of seconds.

Hannah slid her hands into his. "I've had a lot of time to think about things."

He grinned when his eyes searched her face and found hope. "And?"

She felt the tears brimming again, but this time they were happy tears. "And, yes," she said, finding her courage. "The answer is yes. I'll marry you and I'll go to Nigeria. We'll have ten babies if that's what you want," she laughed but her smile faded as she gazed sincerely into his eyes. "I want to be with you - forever. No more separations, no more bad decisions. Just you and me."

Josh was looking at her fully, as if he were holding a precious treasure. Then he pulled her to him again and brought his lips to hers, closing the distance and kissing away any uncertainty, any hurt that had ever been between them.

~ THIRTEEN ~

Before she even opened her eyes, the realization of the day's events began sinking in through the haze of sleep still clouding her mind. She was marrying her best friend in a matter of hours. The thought made her brain instantly snap awake as a wave of elation and anxiety rolled through her stomach.

Hannah sat up in bed, daring to look at the clock in fear she'd slept late. The red numbers glared 5:45 and she suddenly realized it was still dark outside. The ceremony was at ten, which meant there were still four agonizing hours of anticipation to endure. Slumping against her headboard, Hannah took a deep breath and stared into the darkness.

This was the last day she'd wake up in her old room. Tonight would find her at Josh's house, in his bed. Blushing even under the cover of the shadows, Hannah glanced at her dresser and saw the familiar shape of the frame holding Josh's photo from that day long ago at the zoo. She hadn't known then that one day she would be his wife.

Now, Hannah realized how crazy she'd been for not seeing it sooner. He'd been a part of her since she was five, and there was no way she could lose an entire portion of herself. While small segments had been chipped away because of bad decisions and choices, Josh was and always had been the one to piece her back together. And in her own way, she did it for him, too. If God had ever created two people more meant to be together, she'd like to meet that perfect pair, Hannah thought with a smile.

Thoughts of him woke a yearning to hear his voice, and she slid out of bed peeked into the hall. Her dad's closed door was proof he was still asleep, so she silently descended the stairs and headed for the phone. Quickly, she dialed Josh's number and waited impatiently, the ringing so loud it seemed to cut through the silence.

"Hey," came Josh's groggy hello.

160

"I didn't wake you, did I?" Hannah asked quietly as she slipped into a kitchen chair.

"Nah, I barely slept."

"Me either. You nervous?"

She heard him chuckle. "Not really. Just ready to have you all to myself."

Hannah got a quick mental picture of him, lying on his side, head propped on a fist, and realized that this time tomorrow, she'd be there, snuggled up beside him. "Me too," she said, trying to keep her attention focused on the conversation. "I feel like I did in high school, sneaking downstairs to call you."

"Few more hours, baby, and then it's just you and me."

Suddenly the kitchen light flicked on, blinding her. Hannah covered her eyes and moaned.

"Thank goodness," she mumbled, aiming a playful frown at her father, who stood grinning at her. "See you soon, Josh."

"Busted, huh?" he said, laughing. She couldn't help but laugh, too. "See you at the church." Then, tenderly, he added, "I love you."

"I love you, too," she said, aware that her dad could hear from his spot in the doorway.

"Good morning, Mr. Eavesdropper," she teased as she hung up. "Did you sleep well?"

Still grinning ear to ear, Michael tightened the belt on his robe. "Isn't it against some wedding rule to talk to the groom before the ceremony?" He rummaged in a cupboard for the can of coffee

Smiling, Hannah shook her head. She'd never seen her father more excited, and it had been a long, long time since he looked as genuinely happy. His merry grin, coupled with his rumpled hair and lopsided glasses, reminded her of a boy on Christmas morning. "No. The rule is the groom can't see the bride before the ceremony," she corrected, filling the coffeepot with water.

Michael scooped grounds into the filter. "I'll bet you can't wait to be out of your old man's house."

She stood beside him; lay her head on his shoulder. "I'll bet you can't wait to get me out of here." A long, wistful sigh punctuated her sentence. "I'm going to miss you like crazy, Dad but I have to admit it'll feel so good to start acting like an adult for a change." She poured water into the coffee maker's reservoir while her dad slid the basket of grounds into place. They hit the on button at the same moment, and snickered as the pot began sizzling and steaming, and the aromatic scent of fresh-brewed coffee filled the air.

"So, how are you this morning?" he asked, one eye narrowed as he gave her a paternal once-over. "Nervous?"

Hannah breathed deep and leaned against the counter. "Not really. At least, not yet." She hugged herself, then added, "But give me a couple hours, and I'll be singing a different tune."

A soft chuckle sighed from his lips. "Well, we have time, so how about we whip up some breakfast to celebrate?"

He grabbed the box of pancake mix as Hannah got out the griddle. "Celebrate what?" she asked, moving to the fridge for eggs. "Me getting married or finally leaving the house?"

Michael laughed. "You might be celebrating your departure but I'm not, hon. I'll miss you."

Watching as he carefully measured the mix, Hannah felt a pang of sadness. It was obvious he was happy for her, but when she left, he'd be alone. Again. How hard that must have been on him while she was in college. This time, though, she wouldn't abandon him as she had four years ago. Instead, she'd make every effort to include him in her life, and show him how grateful she was for everything he'd done.

For the first time since she'd made her decision to go with Josh to Nigeria, Hannah felt herself questioning whether she was doing the right thing. But she belonged with her husband. She'd stay in touch with her dad, thanks to the Internet.

The thought of Josh warmed her heart, and she felt the heat of a blush creep into her cheeks as butterflies bounced in her stomach. Yes, she was doing the right thing, by both of her favorite men.

While they cooked, Hannah kept the conversation light. This would be the last breakfast she'd share with her father for a while, so while he flipped the pancakes, she stirred the scrambled eggs and poked at bacon, sizzling in a third skillet. She committed their happy banter to memory, knowing there would be plenty of time to regret all the times like these she had wasted, behaving like a pouty teenaged girl. This wasn't a day for regrets or heartache. It was her wedding day, the start of a whole new life for her dad, herself, and Josh.

~ * ~

"How do I look?" Hands trembling, Hannah smoothed her skirt.

Olivia, Shawna, and Erin stood dreamy-eyed around her in a circle, dabbing at tears.

"Honey," Olivia said, voice full of emotion, "you look gorgeous."

Hannah turned to the mirror for one last glance. In moments, it would be time to take her place at the back of the church. Staring at her reflection, she blinked back the hot tears that threatened to smear her makeup. An hour from now, she'd be Josh's wife with all the responsibilities of a full-grown woman. She prayed God would guide her, because she wanted to get this right, wanted to be the spouse her husband deserved and a daughter her father could be proud of.

She hardly recognized the woman in the mirror, who stood tall and proud in a regal ivory gown. Gone was the look of fear and apprehension she'd seen every morning of her life, for far too many years. In its place, an expression of awareness that came from making the right choices for the right reasons, and the right people. This was no terrified girl who looked back at her but a lovely self-assured young woman who was loved, and loved deeply, by two of the finest men God ever created.

Her fingers played with tiny sparkling beads that lined the scooped neckline as Olivia fastened the last of the delicate pearl buttons that went from neck to waist, she said, "Oh. Hannah, you look like a princess. Josh is such a lucky guy." She fussed with shining strands that framed Hannah's face, and then tapped the loose bun at the nape of her neck.

"I don't know if I've seen a prettier bride."

Hannah's bouquet, thanks to Michelle, was a work of art. She'd assembled white irises, accentuated with pink hyacinths, and tied them together with a wide satin ribbon. Minuscule gems glinted on the flower petals, making them glimmer with Hannah's every movement.

"You ready, girl?" Erin asked, giving her wrist a gentle squeeze.

Hannah nodded, then looked at the reflections of her friends. They grinned back for a moment and then burst into gales of laughter and squeals of excitement. They hurried Hannah out the door, where Michael stood running a finger under his collar. The girls each gave her one last hug, then sidled into the sanctuary.

"Sweetie," Michael said, his face aglow with love and pride as he took her hands in his. "You look... you're... you're so beautiful."

She stood on tiptoe to kiss his cheek. "Thanks, Dad. And you look pretty handsome, yourself," she said, smiling.

"I can't believe I'm walking my little girl down the aisle." Glancing toward the big entry doors, he shook his head.

Hannah sucked in a deep breath, and then let it out slowly. "I can't believe it, either."

The pounding strains of *The Wedding March* blasted

as the doors leading into the church slowly opened. Michael looked down at her and poked out his elbow, smiling past the unshed tears that shimmered in his eyes. "Ready?"

Hannah couldn't speak. Her heart filled with love for this wonderful man who stood beside her. Josh had big shoes to fill, she thought, slipping her hand through the crook of his arm. "Ready as I'll ever be."

"Then let's go," he said, taking the first step. As they passed each pew, guests stood. Some waved. Others smiled. A few dabbed tissues to their eyes.

Hannah was aware of the whispers, of the hundreds of eyes focused on her, but all she could see was Josh, standing at the end of the aisle. The sight of him took her breath away. She met his eyes, and sensed that he was drawing her near with the power of his love. He smiled, making her knees go weak, and winked, making her heart dance.

When at last she and her dad reached the altar, Michael stopped and, bending, gave her a kiss on the cheek before releasing her, so she could claim her spot next to Josh. He then made his way to the pulpit to begin the ceremony.

Hannah turned slightly to face her husband-to-be. "You look so handsome," she whispered.

"And you," Josh said, beaming, "look absolutely gorgeous."

"Family and friends," Michael began, "we welcome you today to witness the marriage of Josh and Hannah. You have shared and contributed to their lives in the past, and by witnessing their marriage ceremony today, Josh and Hannah ask you to share in their future.

"Marriage is a promise, made in the hearts of two people who love each other, which takes a lifetime to fulfill. Within the circle of its love, marriage encompasses all life's most important relationships. A wife and a husband are each other's lover, teacher, listener, critic, and best friend."

As her father spoke, Hannah glanced at her soon-to-be life mate, finding it hard to believe it had taken her so long to understand how much he meant to her. All this time she had a man that thought the world of her right in front of her nose. Without a doubt in her mind, Hannah knew Josh would always love and respect her, that he'd make a loving husband and father, that he'd always be her closest and dearest friend. How could she have ever looked anywhere else for the man of her dreams?

"The bride and groom have prepared their own vows," she heard her father say.

Hannah and Josh turned, faced one another, and linked hands. Josh looked deep into Hannah's eyes for a long, silent moment. And then he said, "I, Josh Reynolds, take you, Hannah Sinclair, to be my wife. Already I've been blessed to share my life with you, from our childhood to this day. As my best friend, you've seen me through countless ups and downs, through life's disappointments and victories, through storms and clear days, through separations and reunions. I couldn't imagine sharing those times with anyone else. Today, I give you my hand and my heart, and pray that my love will always be a safe haven for you. I've always loved you, I always will."

Hannah smiled through joyous tears. "And I, Hannah Sinclair, take you, Josh Reynolds to be my husband. You have made me into the woman I am today. You've been by my side for as long as I can remember. You've held me up through the worst times in my life, and have never been selfish or withholding with your love. I love you for being my best friend, a shoulder to lean on, a confidant and safe place, and a role model to so many people, including me. I am so blessed to be able to spend the rest of my life with you, through the good times and the bad, side-by-side. I pray I'll always be for you what you've been for me, and I promise to always love you."

There was a moment of silence, punctuated by a few sniffles from the ladies of the congregation. Then Michael turned to Josh. "Josh," came his clear, deep voice, "do you take Hannah to be your wife? Will you love, honor, and cherish her, in good times and in bad, and do you promise to stay true to her as long as you both shall live?"

Without hesitation, Josh replied, "I do," then gently slid the ring onto her finger.

Facing Hannah, her father said, "Hannah, do you take Josh to be your husband? Will you love, honor, and cherish him, in good times and in bad, and do you promise to stay true to him as long as you both shall live?"

Hannah slipped the silver band onto Josh's finger and whispered, "I do."

With a grin, Michael closed his prayer book and said in a full, sure voice, "Then with the power vested in me by God, I now pronounce you man and wife. You may kiss the bride."

Time seemed to move slowly, ever-so-slowly as Josh slipped his arms around her and pulled her close, so close that not even the slightest hint of a breeze could have passed between them. Looking deep into her eyes, he nodded, then kissed her, long and tender, and she knew he was telling her in that moment that everything he'd said, every word of his vows, had been the pure and honest truth.

Those gathered to help them share this glorious moment got to their feet, whistling and applauding, sighing and laughing. And when they turned to face the friends and family who cheered them on, Hannah sent a silent prayer of thanks heavenward.

~ * ~

Hannah smiled down at the glittering diamond on her finger as she traced the silver band around Josh's. Here she was, Mrs. Josh Reynolds. Hannah Reynolds. How strange, but how wonderful it felt on her tongue and sounded in her ears.

"What are you grinning about?" Josh asked, squeezing her hand.

Some things, she decided, should be kept locked inside a woman's heart. This was one of those, Hannah thought. "Oh, nothing."

Her dad walked briskly up to them, his face flushed from rushing to park the car while they took care of their luggage and paperwork. "You got everything? Your passports, visas, cash?"

"Yes, Dad. We've gone over it a hundred times. It's all here." Hannah swallowed the lump of regret that ached in her throat. It'd been hard enough for him to let her go to college. But saying goodbye as she headed off to Africa? She prayed that God would watch over him, keep him safe, and provide him with plenty of companionship while she was gone. Hannah understood only too well why his bright, bustling demeanor, leading up to the wedding, suddenly turned quiet and thoughtful. He'd barely said a word, driving her and Josh to the airport, and she knew he was worried about them going so far from home, going to a strange and foreign place with no one but each other.

Michael pulled the hanky from his back pocket and wiped his glistening forehead. "I don't mean to imply you guys are inept. I'm just—"

Hannah gripped his hands. "I know, Dad, and I love you for it." Then she felt her throat close up, because this was goodbye. Their suitcases had long ago been taken to the airplane, she and Josh had checked in, and the clock was ticking. In moments, they'd leave Michael, and Illinois, for a long time.

Her dad didn't even try to hide his tears. "Come here," he said, gathering her close. He held her, burying his face in the crook of her neck, for a full minute.

"I'll miss you so much." Hannah's tears streamed down her face.

Her father stepped back, grabbed his handkerchief again and mopped his eyes. Nodding, he turned to Josh, unashamed of his show of emotion. "You take care of my little girl now, you hear?" he said, hugging his new son-in-law.

"You bet," Josh said, patting his father-in-law's back. "She's in good hands."

"I know. Still, you treat her well. Make sure she has everything she needs, and if anything happens, call me, immedia—" The boarding call interrupted him, and looking miserable, Michael gave them each a final hug.

Hannah and Josh walked toward their gate. "I'll write and call every chance I get," she promised as she prayed like crazy she could wait until they were safe inside the plane before the real crying began. The last thing her dad needed right now, she knew, was to see her a blubbering, quivering mess.

She cast one last glance in his direction, returned his slow wave, and then entered the long tube that connected the terminal to the aircraft. "I'm going to see his sad face in my dreams for weeks," she confessed, leaning into Josh. "I know," he said, squeezing her hand. "I know."

A familiar sense of uncertainty about the future pinged in her head, but Hannah wasn't afraid, because this time, she wouldn't face things alone. This time, she'd have Josh at her side, doling out love and support and husbandly advice. This time, she'd have a partner to share everything with.

"You all right?" Josh asked, eyeing her worriedly.

Hannah smiled up at him. "Yeah," she said reassuringly. "I'll take it a day at a time."

With that, she resolved to lay to rest her past and look forward to her future. Her second chance not just at love and living, but with God, the Author of second chances.

~ END ~

www.ingramcontent.com/pod-product-compliance
Lightning Source LLC
Chambersburg PA
CBHW060426130626
46555CB00005B/2232